A JESSICA JONES MYSTERY
ANTS

WRITER
GAIL SIMONE

ARTIST/COVERS
PHIL NOTO

LETTERER **VC's CORY PETIT**
ASSISTANT EDITOR **MARTIN BIRO**
ASSOCIATE EDITOR **ANNALISE BISSA**
EDITOR **TOM BREVOORT**

JESSICA JONES CREATED BY **BRIAN MICHAEL BENDIS** & **MICHAEL GAYDOS**

COLLECTION EDITOR **JENNIFER GRÜNWALD** ASSISTANT EDITOR **DANIEL KIRCHHOFFER**
ASSISTANT MANAGING EDITOR **MAIA LOY** ASSOCIATE MANAGER, TALENT RELATIONS **LISA MONTALBANO**
VP PRODUCTION & SPECIAL PROJECTS **JEFF YOUNGQUIST** BOOK DESIGNER **JAY BOWEN**
SVP PRINT, SALES & MARKETING **DAVID GABRIEL** EDITOR IN CHIEF **C.B. CEBULSKI**

THE VARIANTS. Contains material originally published in magazine form as THE VARIANTS (2022) #1-5. First printing 2022. ISBN 978-1-302-94706-4. Published by MARVEL WORLDWIDE, INC., a subsidiary of MARVEL ENTERTAINMENT, LLC. OFFICE OF PUBLICATION: 1290 Avenue of the Americas, New York, NY 10104. © 2022 MARVEL No similarity between any of the names, characters, persons, and/or institutions in this book with those of any living or dead person or institution is intended, and any such similarity which may exist is purely coincidental. **Printed in the U.S.A.** KEVIN FEIGE, Chief Creative Officer; DAN BUCKLEY, President, Marvel Entertainment; DAVID BOGART, Associate Publisher & SVP of Talent Affairs; TOM BREVOORT, VP, Executive Editor; NICK LOWE, Executive Editor, VP of Content, Digital Publishing; DAN BUCKLEY, President, Marvel Entertainment; DAVID GABRIEL, VP of Print & Digital Publishing; SVEN LARSEN, VP of Licensed Publishing; MARK ANNUNZIATO, VP of Planning & Forecasting; JEFF YOUNGQUIST, VP of Production & Special Projects; ALEX MORALES, Director of Publishing Operations; DAN EDINGTON, Director of Editorial Operations; RICKEY PURDIN, Director of Talent Relations; JENNIFER GRÜNWALD, Director of Production & Special Projects; SUSAN CRESPI, Production Manager; STAN LEE, Chairman Emeritus. For information regarding advertising in Marvel Comics or on Marvel.com, please contact Vit DeBellis, Custom Solutions & Integrated Advertising Manager, at vdebellis@marvel.com. For Marvel subscription inquiries, please call 888-511-5480. **Manufactured between 12/30/2022 and 1/31/2023 by SEAWAY PRINTING, GREEN BAY, WI, USA.**

10 9 8 7 6 5 4 3 2 1

1

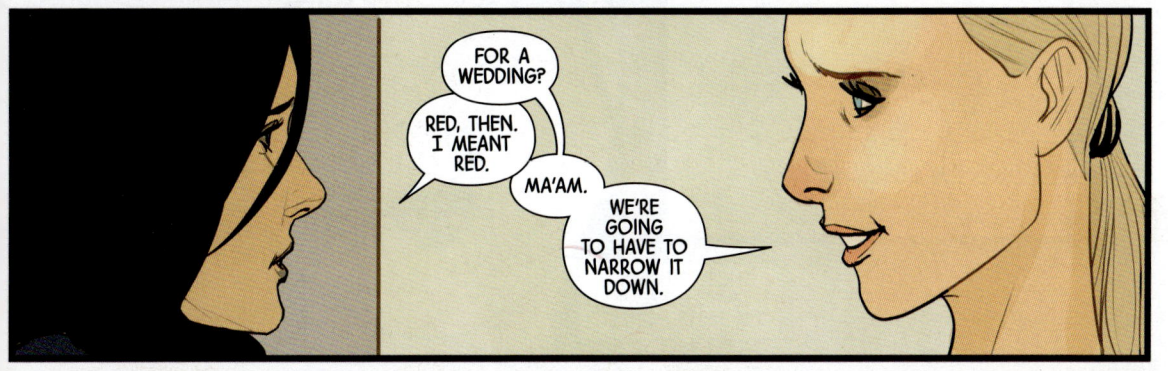

I USED TO HANG HERE.

HELL, I PRACTICALLY LIVED IN THIS PLACE.

LONG CONVERSATIONS LEADING NOWHERE.

LINGERING BECAUSE I DIDN'T KNOW HOW TO BE ALONE AND I COULDN'T STAND TO ACTUALLY *BE* AROUND ANYONE.

UNLESS I WAS IN A PARTICULARLY BLACK MOOD. OR HORNY.

WHICH I ALWAYS WAS.

SAME THING, SAME DAMN THING.

BAD INPUT, BAD OUTCOME.

UNTIL LUKE.

BEAUTIFUL, ENDLESS LUCAS CAGE.

STOMPING GROUNDS

I REMEMBER WE WERE GOING TO BE MARRIED. I WANTED TO BE ENDLESS AND BEAUTIFUL FOR HIM, A LITTLE.

JUST FOR ONE DAY.

I, UH... I NEED SOME STUFF. LIPSTICK, I GUESS. I'M GETTING MARRIED.

THAT'S *WONDERFUL*. WHAT COLOR WERE YOU THINKING?

GEEZ, I DON'T KNOW. BLACK...?

FOR A WEDDING?

RED, THEN. I MEANT RED.

MA'AM. WE'RE GOING TO HAVE TO NARROW IT DOWN.

I ASKED HER NAME AND SHE SAID BRINJA, LIKE IT WAS THE MOST COMMON NAME IN THE WORLD.

THIS WAS HER PLACE OF POWER, LIKE LATVERIA FOR LIPSTICK AND $400 BOTTLES OF JANET VAN DYNE'S SIGNATURE SCENT.

WHICH WAS CALLED *"WINSOME,"* BY THE WAY.

I COULD LITERALLY *FEEL* HER BEGIN TO TAKE PITY ON ME.

NOT ENTIRELY UNWELCOME, IF I'M BEING HONEST.

For Luke, for us, I'd be her pet project for a while.

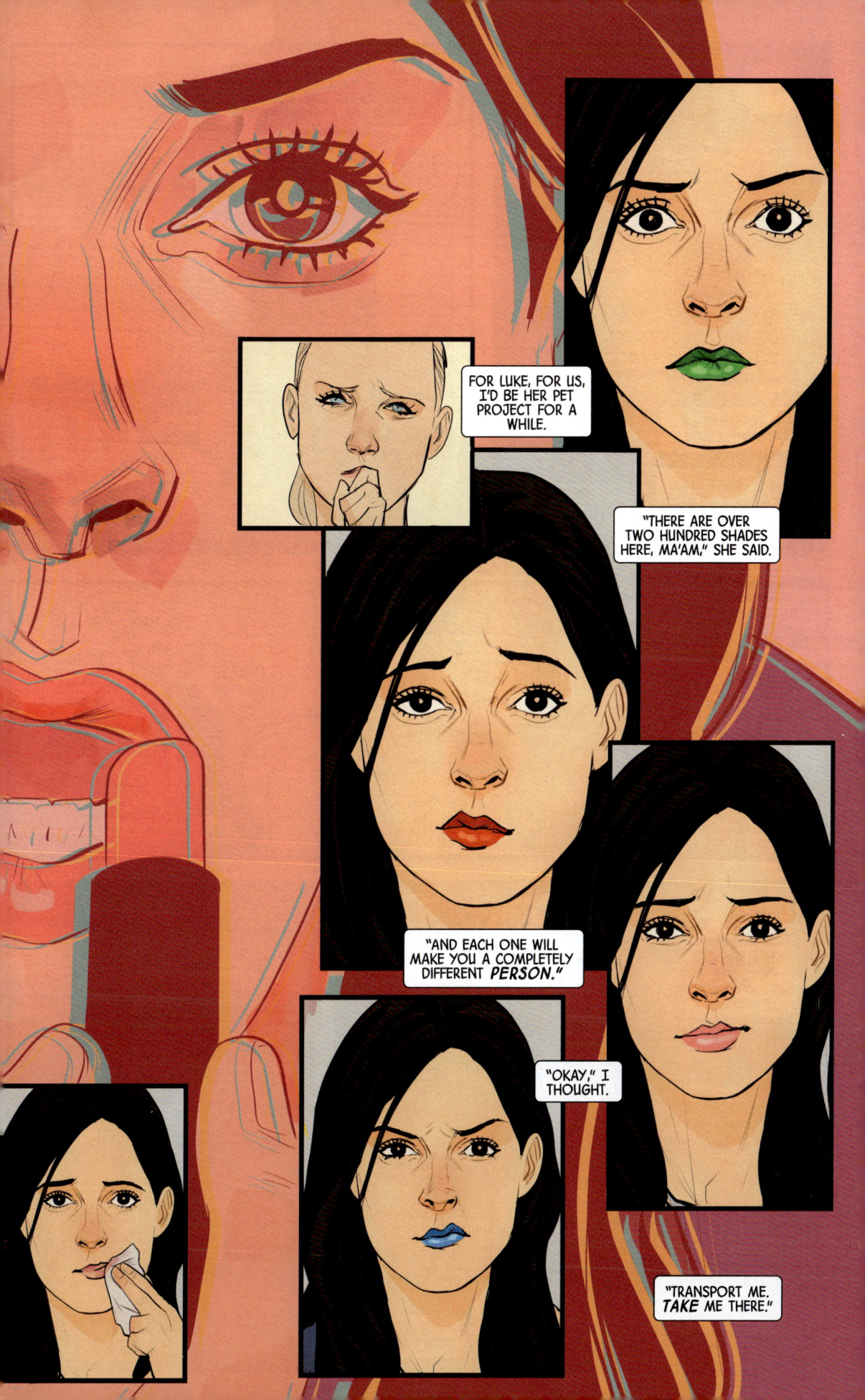

"There are over two hundred shades here, ma'am," she said.

"And each one will make you a completely different *person*."

"Okay," I thought.

"Transport me. *Take* me there."

HUH.

THE COFFEE SHOP... THOUGHT I SAW...

NEVER MIND.

THESE *HEADACHES* LATELY.

IT TOOK ALMOST HALF AN HOUR. I'M SURE SHE CAUGHT FLAMING HELL FROM HER SUPERVISOR, WASTING ALL THAT TIME FOR ONE PALTRY SALE.

LISTEN, I WANT TO THANK YOU--

OH, NO, MA'AM. YOU'RE NOT GETTING AWAY THAT EASY.

IN HIGH SCHOOL, I ACTIVELY AVOIDED THE PRETTY, POPULAR PRINCESSES.

THIS TIME... I DON'T KNOW. NOT SO TOUGH.

I'M SO HAPPY FOR YOU.

GO BE HAPPY FOR YOU TOO. OKAY?

MIGRAINE.

IT ALWAYS FEELS LIKE SPIN-ART MADE OF NEEDLES.

ARE YOU ALL RIGHT, MISS? DO YOU NEED--?

I'M GOOD. I'M PERFECT. THANK YOU.

"WHAT COLOR WERE YOU THINKING?"

GEEZ, I DON'T KNOW.

BLACK...?

MISS!

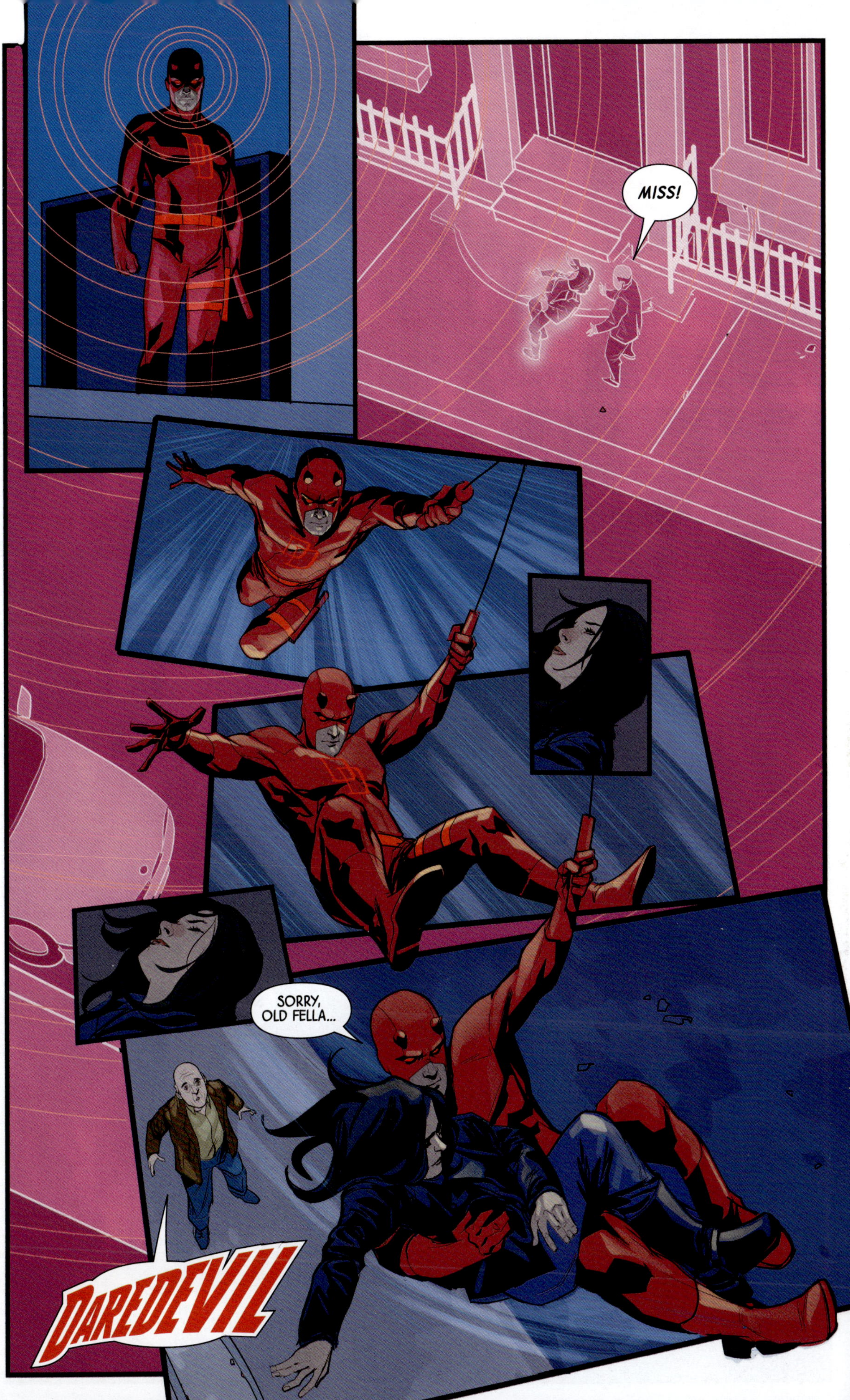
MISS!
SORRY, OLD FELLA...
DAREDEVIL

...BUT I NEVER MISS.

JESSICA. IT'S MATT. YOU PASSED OUT.

DAMN. THIRD TIME IN TWO DAYS.

YOU QUIT DRINKING COFFEE.

YEAH. WAIT. YOU CAN SENSE THAT ON ME?

I CAN. IT'S COMPLICATED.

BUT ALSO, YOU'VE BEEN STARING AT THAT COFFEE PLACE LIKE A DOG WATCHES THANKSGIVING SUPPER. TWO DAYS NOW.

WOULD YOU BELIEVE ME IF I SAID IT WAS FOR A P.I. GIG?

I WOULD. MOSTLY AS A COURTESY, JESSICA.

HAVING A FRIEND YOU CAN'T LIE TO IS A BIT OF A PAIN IN THE ASS, IF I'M BEING HONEST.

I SWEAR, IF YOU SAY YOU'RE BRINGING THE DEFENDERS BACK TOGETH--

I'M NOT.

IT'S MARIA. SHE NEEDS YOU AT THAT HEARING.

LISTEN TO HIM, IN HIS RIDICULOUS COCOON OF CONFIDENCE.

DON'T PUSH ME, MATT.

WE'RE FRIENDS. BUT THERE ARE LIMITS.
SHE HAS NO ONE.
NO ONE BUT US.
WELL, THEN MAYBE MISS PRISS SHOULDN'T HAVE BURNED HER HOUSE DOWN WITH HER FAMILY STILL IN IT, YOU THINK?
THERE'S NO ONE ELSE, JESS.
HE KNOWS. HE KNOWS HE'S WON.
DAMMIT.
"MORNING BLUSH." THAT'S WHAT I PICKED.
EXCUSE ME?
IT WAS GIRLY. PINK. EXTRA LEVELS OF GIRLY.
OKAY.
I'LL BE THERE.
YOU SAY, "I KNOW" AND I'LL BASH YOUR FACE IN FOR YOU, MATT.
...
SO NOTED.
MORNING BLUSH.
SO.
WANT A RIDE HOME?
WANT A BUNCH OF THROW-UP ON YOUR SUIT?

Panel 1: "TOMORROW MORNING, JESSICA. DON'T SCOWL. WEAR SOMETHING LESS SCARY, PLEASE."

"SOME OF THAT COMMUNITY, EVEN SOME AVENGERS... YOU WONDER WHY THEY DO WHAT THEY DO. WHAT THEY *REALLY* GET OUT OF IT."

NOT HIM. NOT MATT.

Panel 2: WHEN THE BLIND GUY HATES YOUR OUTFIT. *HUH.*

MAYBE I NEED TO SEE BRININA AGAIN.

Panel 3: LUKE. THE MOUNTAIN I CLIMB. ENDLESS. PERFECT. AND YET--

Panel 4: --THAT NIGHT, FOR THE FIRST TIME IN MONTHS...

Panel 5: ...I DREAM OF *HIM*. AND THE WORLD'S UGLIEST ANNIVERSARY.

KILLGRAVE.

AND SLEEP IS A MEAN *BASTARD* THE REST OF THE NIGHT.

SO BAD THAT EVEN THE MORNING SUN LOOKS HATEFUL.
OMPING G S
STOM GR
JESSICA! WE MISSED YOU, SWEETIE!
STOMPING GROUNDS
MORE
...
I DON'T SEE HOW.
THE USUAL, RIO.
ARE YOU SURE? I THOUGHT YOU-- NEVER MIND, I GOT THIS.
HEY, IF IT'S GOOD ENOUGH FOR PRESIDENTS AND POETS, RIGHT?
THEY WERE BACK AGAIN. THEY WANT MORE *MONEY.*
JESSICA, I CAN'T PAY IT. YOU GOTTA HELP.
WHO WANTS MONEY, AGAIN?
WHO'S MAKING YOU PAY PROTECTION?
YOU *KNOW* WHO. I *TOLD* YOU. THAT'S WHAT I'M *PAYING* YOU FOR.
HAMMERHEAD.

STOMPING GROUNDS
NOW, RIO, YOU AIN'T CASTING NO *ASPERSIONS* ON MY GOOD NAME, ARE YOU?
I'D HATE TO THINK WE'RE NOT GONNA BE *FRIENDS* NO MORE.
YOU KNOW, I BEEN THINKING.
HOW ABOUT ONE OF YOUR CUSTOMERS GETS HER FACE BURNED, LIKE, REAL BAD. MAYBE THAT'LL OPEN THOSE STINGY POCKETS.
I MEAN, REAL, *REAL* BAD. HOW'D THAT BE FOR A MONDAY MORNIN'?
MAYBE *THIS* LITTLE STORM CLOUD, *HUH,* RIO?
WHO'RE *YOU,* LOOKING AT *HAMMERHEAD* LIKE THAT?
WELL.
I'M NOT THE PRESIDENT.
AND TRUTHFULLY, I'M NOT MUCH OF A *POET* EITHER.
AHHHAAAAH!
KRACK
SHE CRACKED MY LEG OPEN!
KILL HER. KILL HER.

SMASH!
GAAHHH!
GKLLK!
THWACK!
FECKLESS BASTARDS. IN MY COFFEE SHOP?
IN MY COFFEE SHOP?
LOOK AT THIS BRILLIANT DISGUISE, RIO.
SNACKS
A DAMN HAT.
DOES THIS SACK OF CRAP LOOK LIKE A MOB BOSS TO YOU?

AMBULANCE. PLEASE. AMBULANCE.

PIPE DOWN, SQUIGGY, 'FORE I FLATTEN YOUR SKULL FOR *REAL.*

THIS ABOUT CLOSES YOUR ACCOUNT, RIO, WOULDN'T YOU SAY?

ANYTHING. ANYTHING YOU WANT, JESSICA.

WOULD IT *KILL YOU* TO GET ME A &#%$@# DANISH?

TURNS OUT, BY CERTAIN STRAIGHT, WHITE GUY STANDARDS...

...MY WHOLE *WARDROBE* IS SCARY.

IT'LL *HAVE* TO DO, MATT.

"--AGAIN, YOU UNDERSTAND THIS IS NOT A TRIAL, MS. SNYDER.

"THIS IS IN FACT AN INFORMAL HEARING TO ASSESS YOUR COMPETENCY TO STAND TRIAL AND YOUR CAPACITY TO ALLOW FOR A PROPER DEFENSE FOR THE SERIOUS ALLEGATIONS AGAINST YOU.

FOURTH COMMUNITY COURTHOUSE

"YOU DO NOT *HAVE* TO SPEAK. DO YOU UNDERSTAND?"

SORRY I'M LATE, MATT.

I UNDERSTAND, YOUR HONOR.

I WANT TO--

I NEED TO TALK ABOUT WHAT HAPPENED.

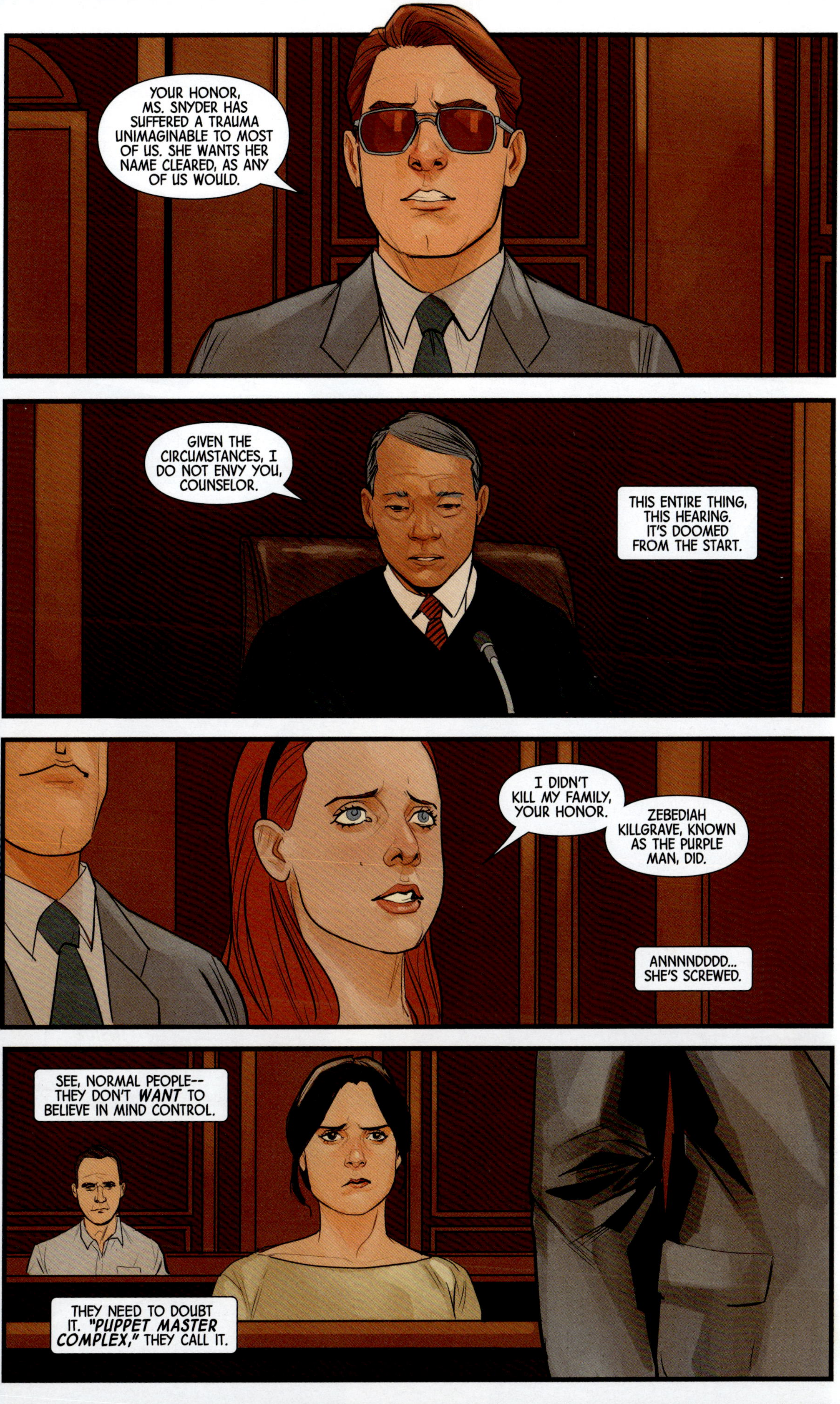
YOUR HONOR, MS. SNYDER HAS SUFFERED A TRAUMA UNIMAGINABLE TO MOST OF US. SHE WANTS HER NAME CLEARED, AS ANY OF US WOULD.
GIVEN THE CIRCUMSTANCES, I DO NOT ENVY YOU, COUNSELOR.
THIS ENTIRE THING, THIS HEARING. IT'S DOOMED FROM THE START.
I DIDN'T KILL MY FAMILY, YOUR HONOR.
ZEBEDIAH KILLGRAVE, KNOWN AS THE PURPLE MAN, DID.
ANNNNDDDD... SHE'S SCREWED.
SEE, NORMAL PEOPLE-- THEY DON'T *WANT* TO BELIEVE IN MIND CONTROL.
THEY NEED TO DOUBT IT. *"PUPPET MASTER COMPLEX,"* THEY CALL IT.

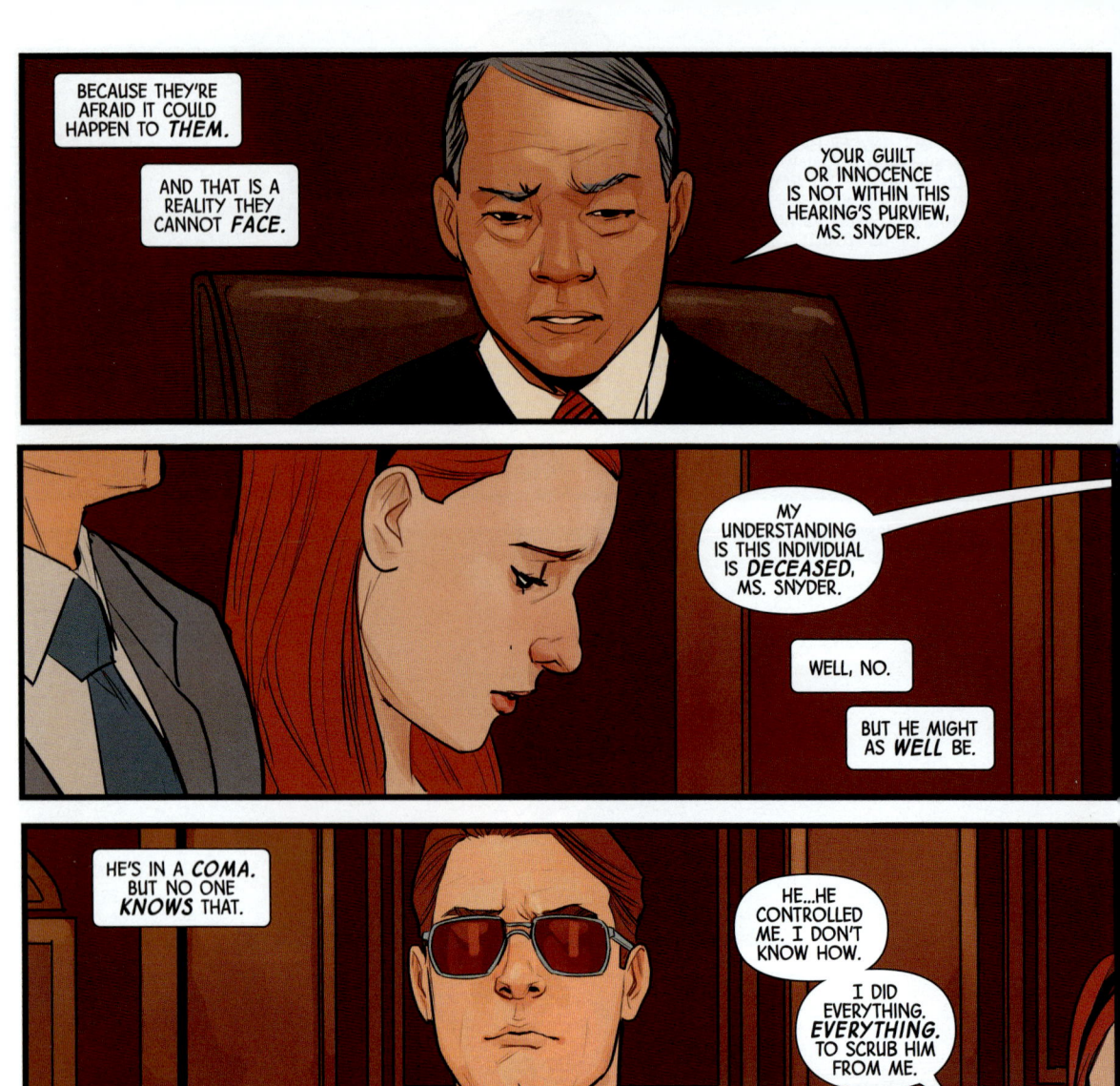

BECAUSE THEY'RE AFRAID IT COULD HAPPEN TO *THEM*.

AND THAT IS A REALITY THEY CANNOT *FACE*.

YOUR GUILT OR INNOCENCE IS NOT WITHIN THIS HEARING'S PURVIEW, MS. SNYDER.

MY UNDERSTANDING IS THIS INDIVIDUAL IS *DECEASED*, MS. SNYDER.

WELL, NO.

BUT HE MIGHT AS *WELL* BE.

HE'S IN A *COMA*. BUT NO ONE *KNOWS* THAT.

HE...HE CONTROLLED ME. I DON'T KNOW HOW.

I DID EVERYTHING. *EVERYTHING*. TO SCRUB HIM FROM ME.

BUT ONE NIGHT, HE WAS JUST...BACK.

INSIDE OF ME. IN MY *HEAD*.

LAUGHING, AS I POURED THE KEROSENE.

LAUGHING.

AND IT GOES JUST AS WE ALL KNEW IT WOULD.
I DON'T EVEN KNOW HOW TO FEEL AT THIS POINT.
SHE WANTS TO TALK TO YOU, JESS.
THE JUDGE OKAY WITH THAT?
HE OWES ME A FAVOR.
IS SHE GONNA SKIP ON THE CHARGES?
NOT THAT BIG A FAVOR.
JESSICA, YOU'RE THE ONLY ONE WHO UNDERSTANDS WHAT SHE'S ALLEGING.
YES. YES, I AM.
AND IT'S MAKING MY KNEES SHAKE SO BAD, I CAN BARELY STAND UP.
SO, YOU, UH...
...YOU WANTED TO SEE ME?
MS. JONES.
JONES-CAGE.
BEFORE HE TOOK YOU...HE TOOK ME.
EVERYTHING HE DID TO YOU--
--HE PERFECTED ON ME FIRST.
THE TORTURE. THE HUMILIATION.

"HE *MARKED* ME. I WAS JUST...SOMEONE WHO ENTERED HIS FIELD OF VISION ONE DAY.

"AND THEN HE WAS IN MY *MIND.* YOU *KNOW.*

"UNTIL ONE DAY... ONE BLESSED, GOD-GIVEN DAY--

"--HE GOT *BORED.* LET ME *GO.*

"WITH A CRANIUM FULL OF *RAZORS* WHERE MY MEMORIES USED TO BE."

KILLGRAVE IS *BEYOND* BEING ABLE TO HURT ANYONE, MARIA.

I'VE SEEN HIM. I *KNOW.*

YOU THINK I'M BEGGING YOU TO HELP ME, MS. JONES-CAGE.

I'M NOT. I'M *WARNING* YOU.

HE LAID A TRAP. A LAND MINE. IN MY *BRAIN.*

I WOULD *NEVER* KNOW PEACE, HE SAID. EVEN AFTER HE LET ME GO.

TEN YEARS TO THE *DAY.*

I HEARD HIS VOICE *AGAIN.*

YOU THINK HE WOULDN'T HAVE PLANTED THE SAME EVIL POISON IN *YOU?*

GET AWAY, JESSICA.

GO SOMEWHERE FAR.

NO.

SHE'S *LYING.*

YOUR *FAMILY.*

STAY AWAY FROM YOUR *FAMILY.*

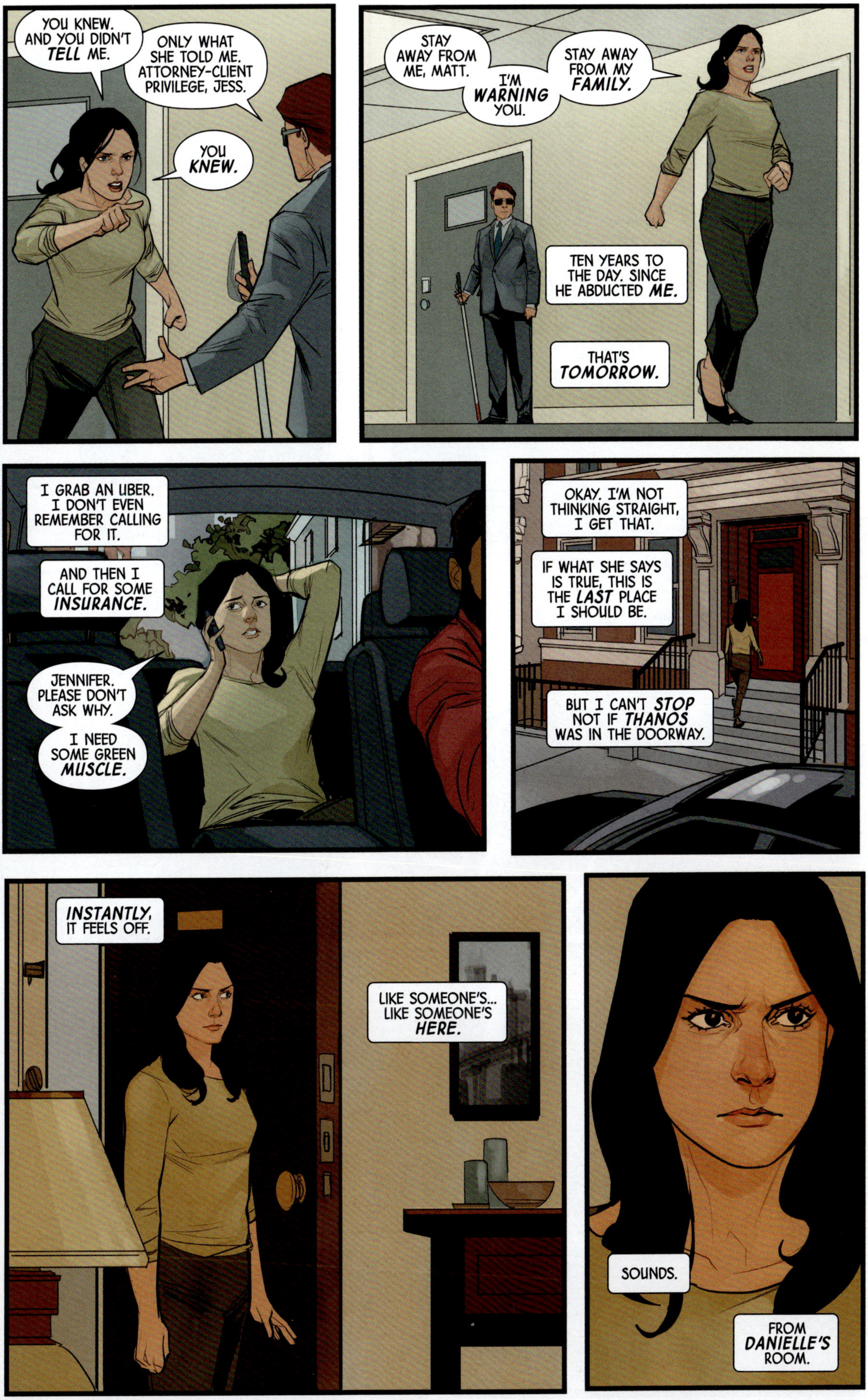
YOU KNEW. AND YOU DIDN'T TELL ME.
ONLY WHAT SHE TOLD ME. ATTORNEY-CLIENT PRIVILEGE, JESS.
YOU KNEW.
STAY AWAY FROM ME, MATT.
I'M WARNING YOU.
STAY AWAY FROM MY FAMILY.
TEN YEARS TO THE DAY. SINCE HE ABDUCTED ME.
THAT'S TOMORROW.
I GRAB AN UBER. I DON'T EVEN REMEMBER CALLING FOR IT.
AND THEN I CALL FOR SOME INSURANCE.
JENNIFER. PLEASE DON'T ASK WHY.
I NEED SOME GREEN MUSCLE.
OKAY. I'M NOT THINKING STRAIGHT, I GET THAT.
IF WHAT SHE SAYS IS TRUE, THIS IS THE LAST PLACE I SHOULD BE.
BUT I CAN'T STOP NOT IF THANOS WAS IN THE DOORWAY.
INSTANTLY, IT FEELS OFF.
LIKE SOMEONE'S... LIKE SOMEONE'S HERE.
SOUNDS.
FROM DANIELLE'S ROOM.

OH. OH, YOU POOR THING, WHOEVER YOU ARE.
YOU BREAK INTO *MY* HOUSE, *MY* DAUGHTER'S ROOM.
ON *THIS DAY.*
WHAT A LOUSY MORNING YOU'RE ABOUT TO *HAVE,* LADY.
WHO...?
THE *DAY* BEFORE THE ANNIVERSARY...IT *CAN'T* BE COINCIDENCE.
SHE'S WITH *HIM.*
CRASH!
ALL RIGHT.
UNGGH.
WHERE'S LUKE? WHERE'S MY *HUSBAND?*
WHERE'S MY *DAUGHTER?*
I'LL TEAR YOUR *HEAD* OFF.
DON'T HAVE A *DOUBT.*

WHAT THE HOLY HELL?
IT'S ME. SHE'S ME.
IS THIS A SKRULL THING OR--?
ACTUALLY...
...WHO CARES?
ALL RIGHT, TWINSIE.
WHAT ARE YOU DOING IN MY HOUSE?
WELL, FOR A START...
...THIS IS MY HOUSE, FREAK.
AND MY WELCOME ISN'T GOING TO BE NEARLY SO SWEET.
WHACK
WHUUK
OW.
YOU BOTH CAN TAKE A HARD TIME-OUT, LADIES.
THAT HURT.

WAIT.

WHAT IN THE WORLD...?

I MEAN, UNLESS YOU WANT TO TRY MESSING WITH **CAPTAIN AMERICA**

CRISIS.

I'M HAVING A CRISIS.

SWELL.

noto

2

FOUR YEARS AGO.

"NOT GONNA LIE, JESS. I MISSED THIS."

"MISSED WHAT, EXACTLY?"

"YOU KNOW. THIS. TALKING IN A DINER. GOOD COFFEE. BEING STARED AT."

"YOU WORE A PLUNGE TOP TO A STAKEOUT, GREER. PRETTY SURE YOU'D GET STARED AT ANYWHERE."

"YEAH, WELL..."

"THEY'RE GOING TO LOOK ANYWAY. I CAN'T CHANGE THAT. SO I MAKE THEM LOOK BECAUSE I *SAID* TO LOOK, YOU KNOW?"

"I ALWAYS FORGET, THESE WOMEN, THESE WARRIORS--"

"--DON'T GET ME WRONG--"

"--THEY PUT SO MUCH PRESSURE ON THEMSELVES. TO BE DANGEROUS *AND* GLAMOROUS."

"HELP YOU LADIES?"

"EIGHT EGGS, PLEASE."

"HOW YOU WANT THEM EGGS COOKED, DARLIN'?"

"DID I SAY ANYTHING ABOUT 'COOKED'?"

ME, I HAVE TWO JACKETS AND ONE'S GOT BLOODSTAINS ON IT.

I REMEMBER ONCE, THE WASP CAUGHT A KID FALLING OFF A COLLAPSING ROOF.

PAPERS RAN A SHOT OF HER BUTT CRACK.

YEAH, I WAS GOING TO ASK ABOUT THAT.

GUY WAS CLEARLY SUPERHUMAN. YOU COULDA *SWUNG* ON OUR BOY.

SOMEONE'S ALWAYS *STARING* AT THEM, THE SHINY WOMEN.

THEY NEVER GET TO FORGET IT.

WELL, WE GOT OUR PEEPER, ANYWAY.

"WORLD'S MIGHTIEST *MOON*," WAS THE CAPTION.

CAN'T DO IT. *WON'T* DO IT.

RIGHT. I DON'T WANT TO TALK ABOUT THIS, TIGRA.

STACK OF PANCAKES, BACON CRISP, PLEASE.

I'VE BEEN SEEN *ENOUGH*.

TOO *MUCH*.

LISTEN, IT'S BEEN FUN, MOONLIGHTING WITH YOU.

I LIKE IT, HONEST.

BUT I HAVE THIS OFFER-- THEY'D TAKE YOU TOO. I KNOW THEY WOULD.

SIEGFRIED AND ROY FINALLY CALL?

THAT WAS MEAN, JESS.

NO FUR OFF *MY* NOSE, BABE.

BUT THAT HESITATION-- IT'S GONNA GET SOMEONE *HURT*.

NO. THEY'RE NEW. THEY'RE CALLED A-FORCE.
GET THIS--ALL GIRLS.
COUPLE A-LISTERS TOO. CAPTAIN MARVEL.
A NEW TEAM WITH CAROL, AND SHE NEVER CALLED ME?
THAT ACTUALLY STINGS A BIT.
YOU COULD BE STRICTLY NONCOMBAT, JESSICA.
GET YOU OUT OF THAT CRAPPY OFFICE.
I LIKE MY CRAPPY OFFICE.
YOU AND ME, JESS.
NO MORE PEEP-FREAKS.
NO MORE GREASY DIVORCE CASES.
MAYBE SEE THE STARS.
GREER. TIGRA.
I HAVE ONE THING IN MY LIFE THAT'S RIGHT. THAT FITS.
I GET IT.
LUKE.
I HAVE LUKE.
LIKE I SAID, I GET IT. I'M HAPPY FOR YOU.
AND YOU'LL BE SAFE HERE.
"SAFE"? IN HELL'S KITCHEN?
YES, SAFE.
WHO'S GONNA HURT YOU HERE--THE DAMN STILT-MAN?
LISTEN.

Panel 1:
"THIS PLACE. THERE'S SOMETHING ABOUT IT."
"I CAN'T EXPLAIN IT IN HUMAN WORDS. IT'S A FEELING AT THE TIP OF MY TAIL."
"BUT THERE'S SOMETHING... SOMETHING *CONCEALED* ABOUT IT."

Panel 2:
"THINK ABOUT IT. WHEN *GALACTUS* OR *ULTRON* SHOWS UP, THEY NEVER COME *HERE*."
"THEY DON'T EVEN KNOW THIS PLACE *EXISTS*."
"IT'S LIKE A *BLIND* SPOT."
"LIKE IT DOESN'T--"
"LIKE WE DON'T--"

Panel 3:
"LIKE WE DON'T MATTER."
"YES. LIKE WE DON'T MATTER."
"BUT WE DO MATTER."

Panel 4:
"YOU MATTER."

Panel 5:
"WHAT I'M WORRIED IS..."
"...WITH THE BIG GUYS, THE SCARY GUYS?"
"DORMAMMU, DOOM, *THOSE* GUYS?"

Panel 6:
"SOME DAY, SOME ROTTEN DAY--"
"--THIS PLACE'LL SHOW UP ON THEIR *RADAR*."

"AND *THAT* DAY, JESSICA JONES...

"...THAT DAY, THEY'LL BURN IT ALL *DOWN*."

NOW.

I SEE WHAT YOU'RE THINKING, LADY. STAND DOWN. I *MEAN* IT.

WEIRD HOW THAT CONVERSATION WITH *TIGRA* FLASHED INTO MY BRAIN RIGHT NOW.

I KNOW WHY THOUGH.

I KNOW WHAT IT'S TRYING TO *TELL* ME.

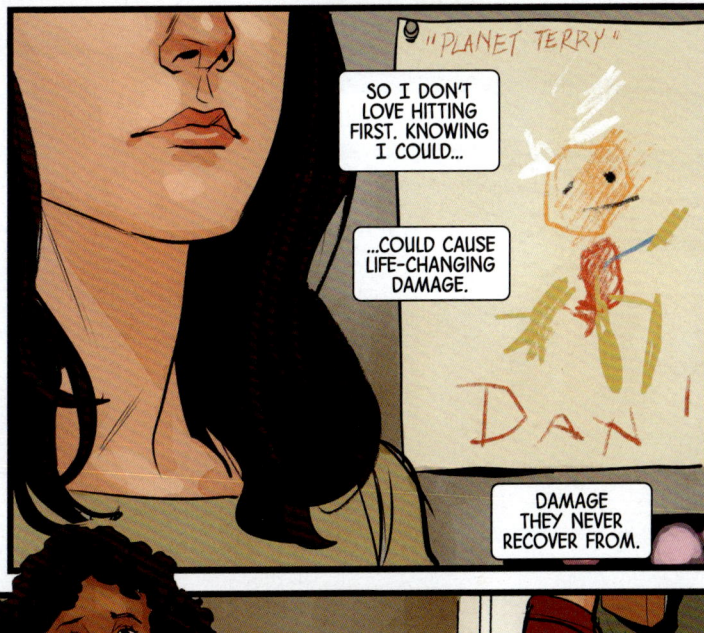

REALLY? CAN YOU TELL WHAT I'M THINKING RIGHT NOW?

IT'S ABOUT WHERE YOU CAN STICK THAT SHIELD.

IT'S REMINDING ME.

OF THOSE EIGHT MONTHS I SPENT UNDER KILLGRAVE'S ABSOLUTE MIND CONTROL.

THE THINGS HE MADE ME DO.

THE PEOPLE HE MADE ME HURT.

WITH MY POWERS.

HE LOVED TO SEE ME WRECK PEOPLE.

SO I DON'T LOVE HITTING FIRST. KNOWING I COULD...

...COULD CAUSE LIFE-CHANGING DAMAGE.

DAMAGE THEY NEVER RECOVER FROM.

BUT THIS IS MY HOME.

MOMMY...?

OH GOD.

DANI.

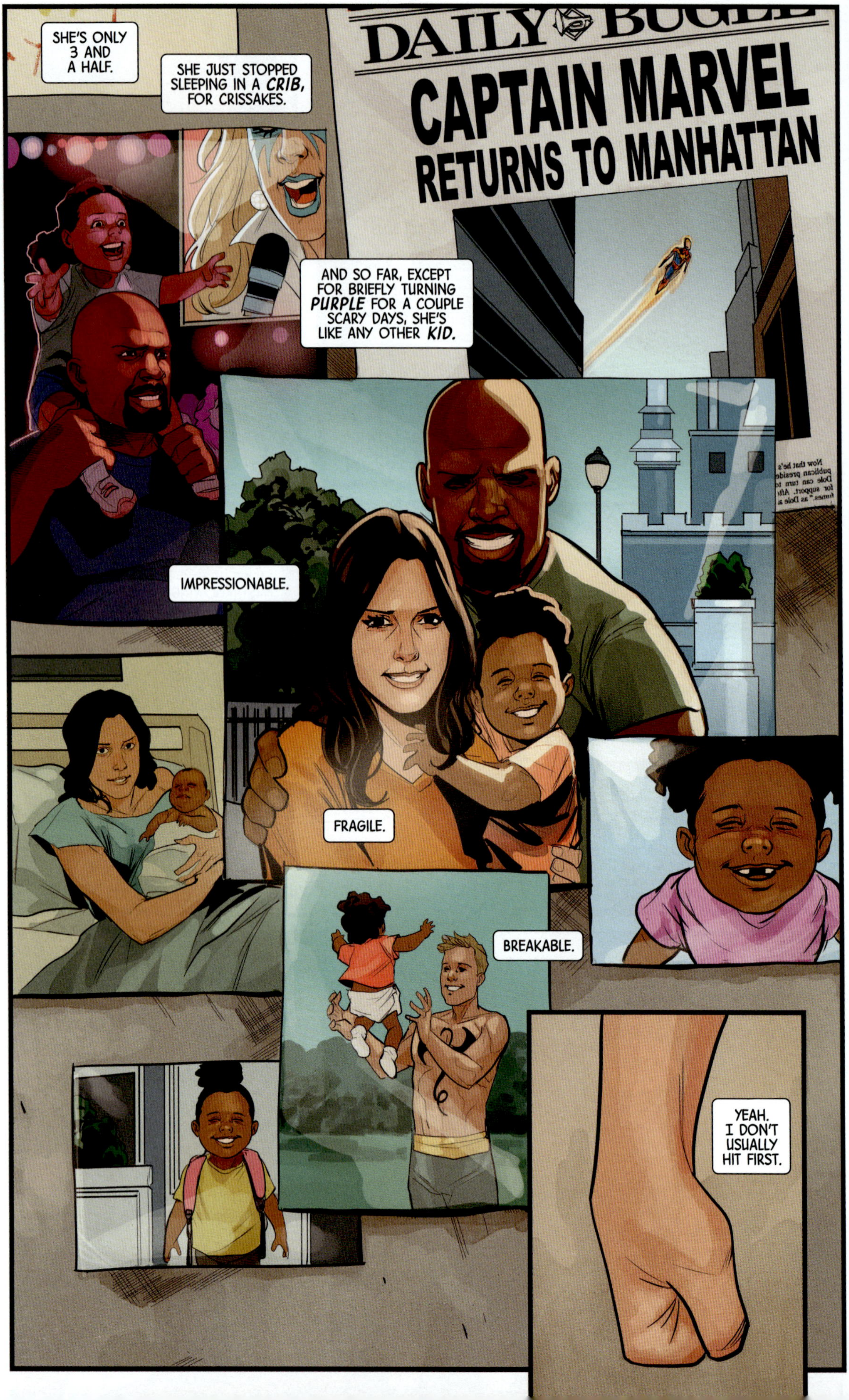
SHE'S ONLY 3 AND A HALF.
SHE JUST STOPPED SLEEPING IN A *CRIB*, FOR CRISSAKES.
DAILY BUGLE
CAPTAIN MARVEL RETURNS TO MANHATTAN
AND SO FAR, EXCEPT FOR BRIEFLY TURNING *PURPLE* FOR A COUPLE SCARY DAYS, SHE'S LIKE ANY OTHER *KID*.
IMPRESSIONABLE.
FRAGILE.
BREAKABLE.
YEAH. I DON'T USUALLY HIT FIRST.

THEN AGAIN.
SOMETIMES I DO.
NEXT ONE, COPYCAT?
NEXT TIME YOU EVEN LOOK AT MY KID?
WE GO BALLS OUT.
ENOUGH. NO MORE WARNINGS.
YOU TWO SCARED MY KID, "CAP."
YOU'RE IN THE MOST DANGEROUS REAL ESTATE IN THE WORLD, YOU KNOW THAT?
WHAT, HELL'S KITCHEN?
NOT SCARED, LADY.
NO. NOT HELL'S KITCHEN.
I MEANT THE SMALL PATCH OF CARPET BETWEEN MY HUSBAND AND HIS DAUGHTER.

OH.
OH.
YEAH.
THAT'S JUST WHAT I WAS THINKING.
BEAUTIFUL.
ENDLESS.
THEY USED TO CALL HIM POWER MAN.
NOT GONNA LIE.
I'VE SHOUTED IT OUT A FEW TIMES IN THE DARK MYSELF.
MOMMY.
AT LEAST SHE KNOWS I'M ME.
WAS HAVING A LITTLE DOUBT ABOUT THAT FOR A SECOND.
JESS, WHAT THE HELL?
NO IDEA.
COME ON, WHILE THEY'RE OUT COLD.

OH. OH NO.
NOT NOW.
JESSICA...?
NOT AGAIN.
TAKE...TAKE DANI...
JESSICA.
JESS.
JESSICAA...
NO.
WHAT THE #$@%?!
HELLO, LITTLE PRINCESS.
NONO NONONO

THE PURPLE MAN.
KILLGRAVE.
DID YOU MISS ME, PET?
NO.
NO.
YOU. YOU'RE IN A COMA. YOU'RE BRAIN-DEAD.
I SAW YOU.
LET'S NOT QUIBBLE.
LET'S JUST BE GRATEFUL I'M BACK, SHALL WE, PET?
EIGHT MONTHS. EIGHT MONTHS.
HE CONTROLLED EVERY MOVEMENT.

YOUR DAUGHTER'S CRYING. HOW SWEET.
SHE LOVES YOU.
YEAH?
YOUR DAUGHTER HATES YOUR GUTS.
IT'S ALMOST MIDNIGHT, SOURPUSS. DO YOU KNOW WHAT THAT MEANS?
TEN YEARS.
TEN YEARS SINCE HE TOOK ME.
SOMETHING IS COMING FOR YOU, JESSICA.
SOMETHING COVETOUS. SOMETHING WANTING.
I CAME TO WARN YOU, MY MUSIC-BOX BALLERINA. BECAUSE I CARE SO DEEPLY, YOU SEE.
OH, AND BY THE WAY...
...HAVE YOU CHECKED ON MARIA?
AAURUUUUOOOFFF!
MOMMY!
MARIA.
MY PHONE.
LUKE.
GET MY PHONE.

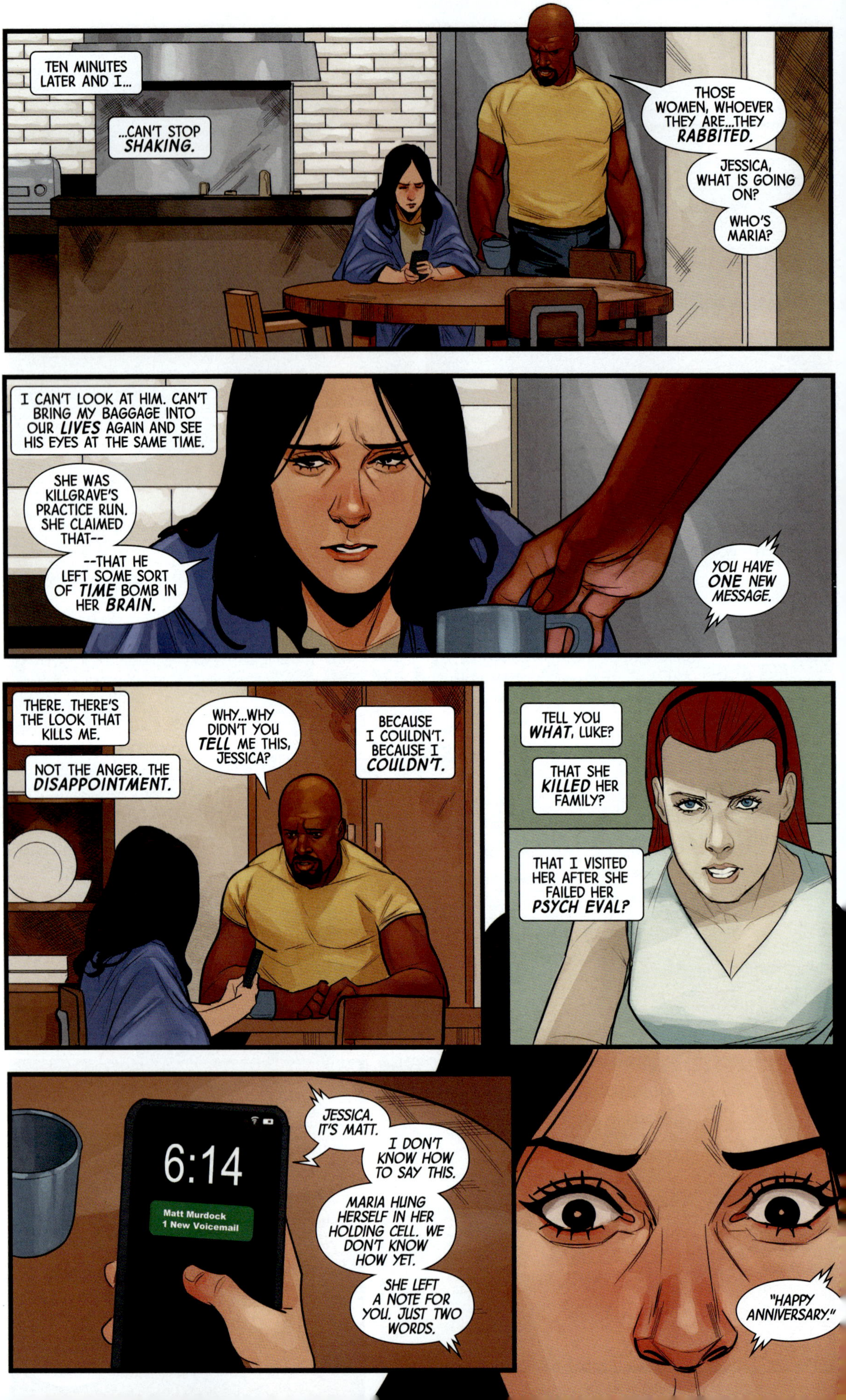
TEN MINUTES LATER AND I...
...CAN'T STOP SHAKING.
THOSE WOMEN, WHOEVER THEY ARE...THEY RABBITED.
JESSICA, WHAT IS GOING ON?
WHO'S MARIA?
I CAN'T LOOK AT HIM. CAN'T BRING MY BAGGAGE INTO OUR LIVES AGAIN AND SEE HIS EYES AT THE SAME TIME.
SHE WAS KILLGRAVE'S PRACTICE RUN. SHE CLAIMED THAT--
--THAT HE LEFT SOME SORT OF TIME BOMB IN HER BRAIN.
YOU HAVE ONE NEW MESSAGE.
THERE. THERE'S THE LOOK THAT KILLS ME.
NOT THE ANGER. THE DISAPPOINTMENT.
WHY...WHY DIDN'T YOU TELL ME THIS, JESSICA?
BECAUSE I COULDN'T. BECAUSE I COULDN'T.
TELL YOU WHAT, LUKE?
THAT SHE KILLED HER FAMILY?
THAT I VISITED HER AFTER SHE FAILED HER PSYCH EVAL?
6:14
Matt Murdock
1 New Voicemail
JESSICA. IT'S MATT.
I DON'T KNOW HOW TO SAY THIS.
MARIA HUNG HERSELF IN HER HOLDING CELL. WE DON'T KNOW HOW YET.
SHE LEFT A NOTE FOR YOU. JUST TWO WORDS.
"HAPPY ANNIVERSARY."

"YOUR FAMILY," SHE SAID.
"STAY AWAY FROM YOUR FAMILY."
JESSICA.
WHAT IS HAPPENING?
YOU HAVE TO LEAVE, LUKE.
TAKE DANI. PACK A BAG AND GO.
NOW.
GO SOMEWHERE I DON'T KNOW. WHERE I CAN'T FIND YOU.
LUKE. IF YOU EVER LOVED ME. IF YOU LOVE ME NOW.
PLEASE.
JUST GO.
AND BECAUSE HE LOVES ME... BECAUSE HE'S LUKE...
HE DOES. NO QUESTIONS, NO ANGRY WORDS.
AND THAT HURTS LIKE I DIDN'T KNOW I COULD STILL HURT.
JEN?
I'M...
I'M IN TROUBLE.

"JESSICA?"

"I'VE BEEN FOLLOWING YOU. I WAS WORRIED. ARE YOU...ARE YOU OKAY?"

"JESSICA...?"

"MATT? MATT?"

"MATT. GOOD GOD IN HEAVEN."

THANK YOU, GOD. THANK YOU, LORD.
THEY SAID, THEY SAID DAREDEVIL WAS A WOMAN NOW.
I THOUGHT...I THOUGHT...
JESSICA, WHAT...?
SHUT UP.
DON'T-- DON'T SAY ANYTHING.
JUST LET ME BREATHE YOU IN.
JES--
SHHH.
HUSH.

I'VE MISSED YOU.
YOU CAN'T POSSIBLY KNOW.
WAIT. OKAY. WAIT.
STOP.
STOP, JESSICA!
WHAT BROUGHT THIS ON?
WE'RE NOT DOING THIS, OKAY?
WHAT ABOUT LUKE?
FOR GOD'S SAKE, WHAT ABOUT YOU?
...
GO AWAY.
GO AWAY BEFORE I HURT YOU.
JESSICA, LET ME HELP--
JESSICA.

OKAY, WE'RE DOING THIS.
READY?
NOT *REALLY.*
GO AHEAD.
SORRY. *SORRY.*
ANYTHING?
I DON'T KNOW.
I GUESS...?
OKAY.
THAT WAS *PRACTICE.*
TELL ME WHEN.
I'LL *TELL* YOU *"WHEN,"* SMARTASS.
WHEN.
WE GOOD, SIS?

WE'RE GOOD.
YOU COULDA PRETENDED TO BE HURT.
OKAY, THEN.
THAT UPPERCUT STUNG A BIT, SORTA.
YOU'RE JUST TRYING TO MAKE ME FEEL BETTER.
WHAT'S WITH THE FF UNIFORM?
YOU SAID HURRY. I GRABBED SOMETHING THAT MIGHT SCARE A BAD GUY A LITTLE.
I DON'T KNOW.
WHAT'S GOING ON, JESS?
I NEED SOMEONE TO WATCH ME, JEN. MAKE SURE I DON'T HURT ANYONE, INCLUDING MYSELF.
SOMEONE I CAN'T JUST PUNCH AND WALK AWAY.
UH-HUH. AND HOW LONG?
TWENTY-FOUR HOURS.
THANK YOU.
BWOOM
WHAT THE HELL WAS THAT?
BOTH OF US HERE AND YOU PULL A GUN?
HOW CUTE.
WHOEVER'S IN MY DAUGHTER'S ROOM...I HAVE A GUN.
AND AN AVENGER.
THAT TOO.
WE'RE COMING IN.

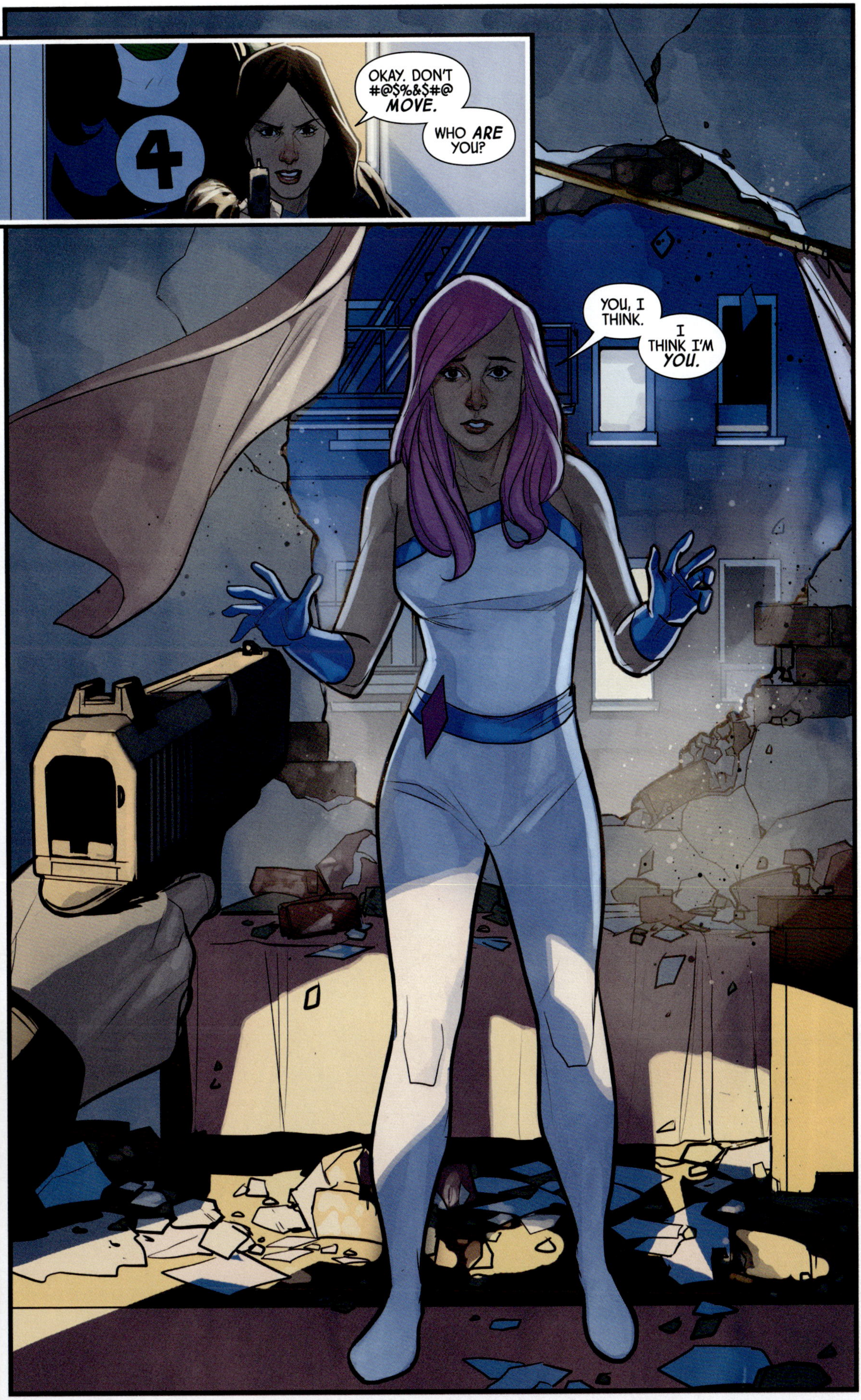
OKAY. DON'T #@$%&$#@ MOVE.
WHO ARE YOU?
YOU, I THINK.
I THINK I'M YOU.

3

"THERE ARE OVER TWO HUNDRED SHADES HERE, MA'AM," SHE SAID.

"AND EACH ONE WILL MAKE YOU A COMPLETELY DIFFERENT *PERSON*."

THE LAST TEN YEARS, MY BRAIN, THE CENTER OF MY *BEING*, HAS BEEN MY ENEMY.

FIRST FEARS, THEN ASSAULT, THEN MEMORY.

WE WERE JUST--

WE WERE JUST STARTING TO BE *FRIENDS* AGAIN.

THEN THIS.

I *CANT*

I *DONT* THINK I CAN TAKE

...

HELP ME

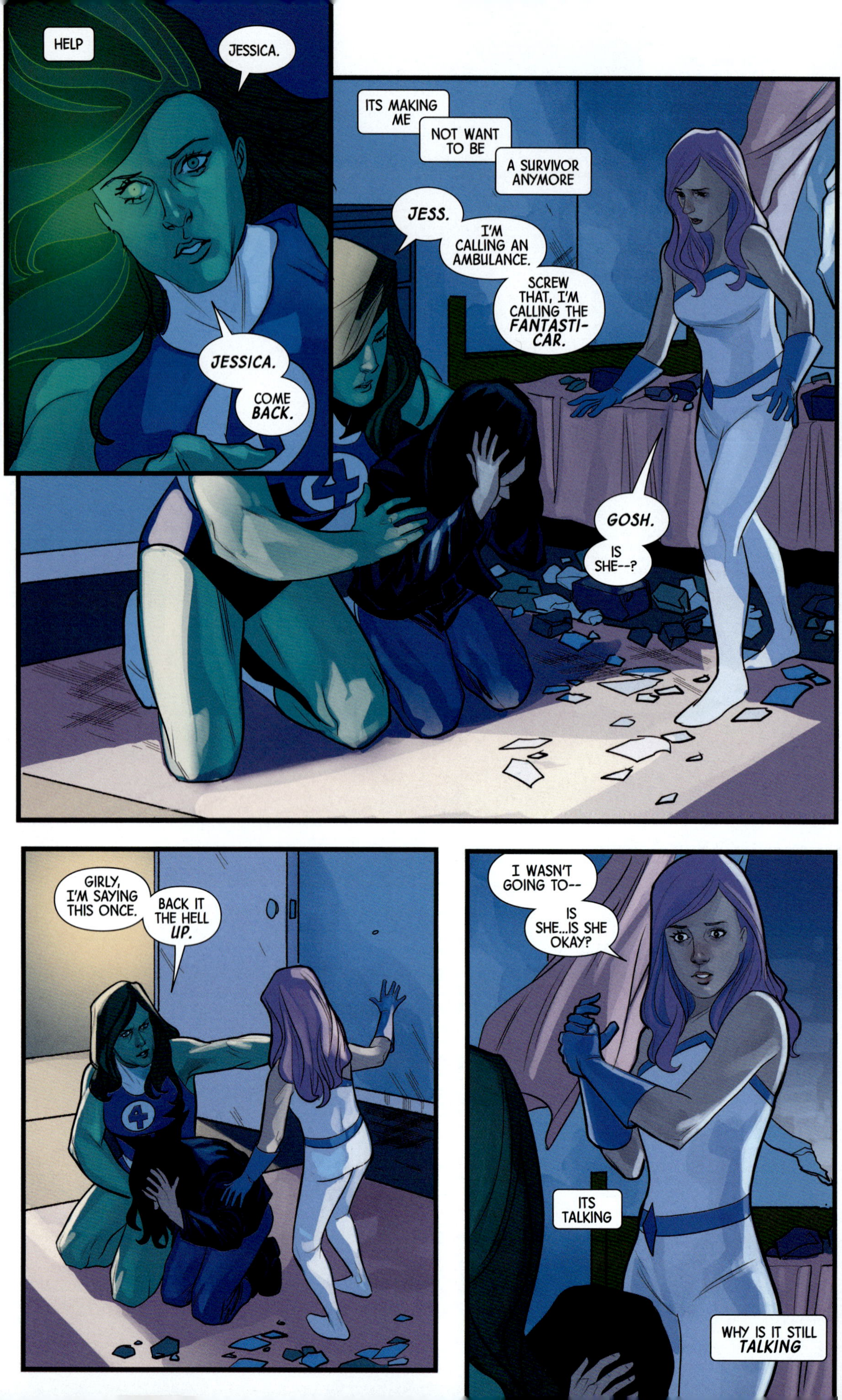
HELP
JESSICA.
JESSICA.
COME BACK.
ITS MAKING ME
NOT WANT TO BE
A SURVIVOR ANYMORE
JESS.
I'M CALLING AN AMBULANCE.
SCREW THAT, I'M CALLING THE FANTASTI-CAR.
GOSH.
IS SHE--?
GIRLY, I'M SAYING THIS ONCE.
BACK IT THE HELL UP.
I WASN'T GOING TO--
IS SHE...IS SHE OKAY?
ITS TALKING
WHY IS IT STILL TALKING

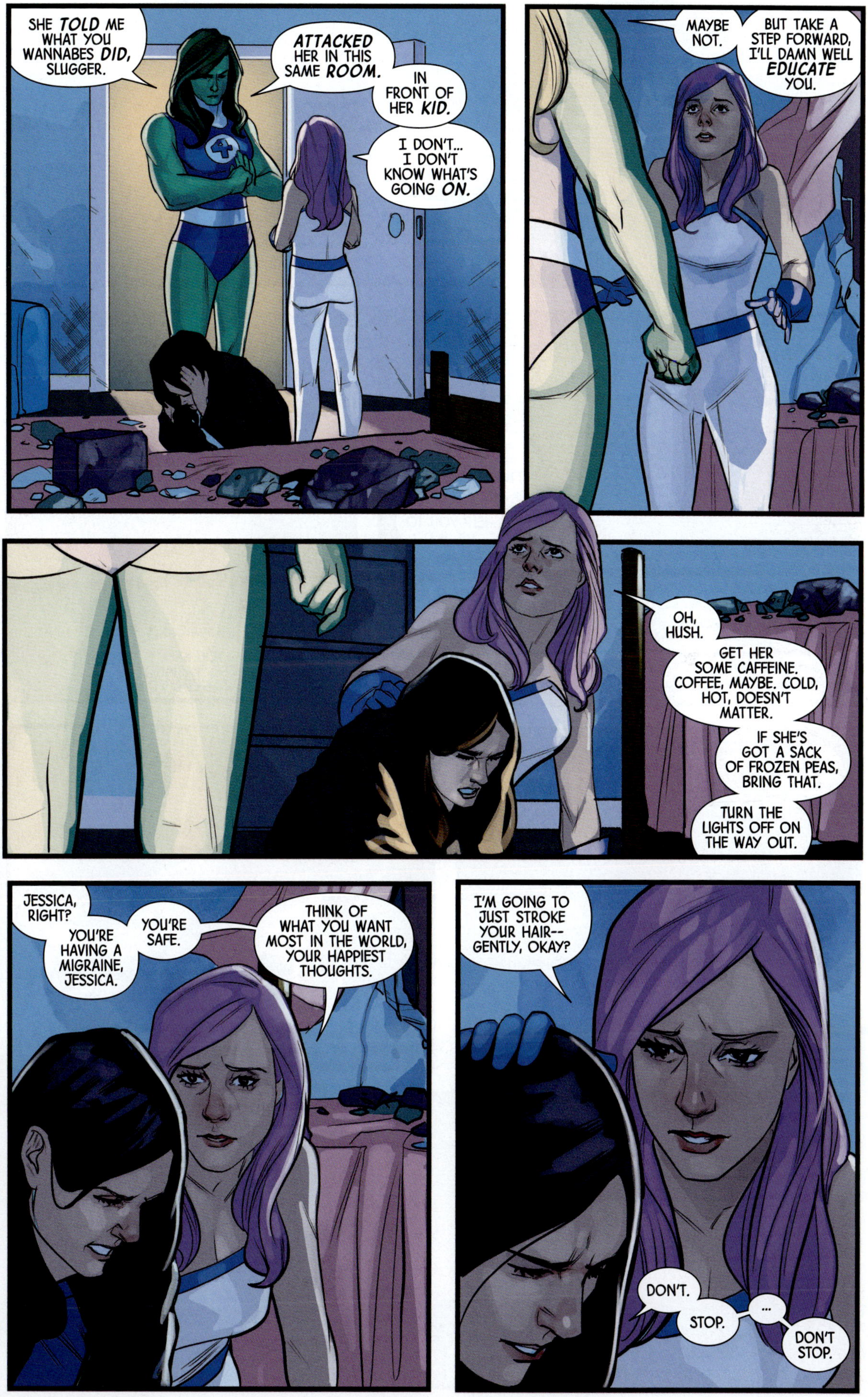

SHE TOLD ME WHAT YOU WANNABES DID, SLUGGER.
ATTACKED HER IN THIS SAME ROOM.
IN FRONT OF HER KID.
I DON'T... I DON'T KNOW WHAT'S GOING ON.
MAYBE NOT.
BUT TAKE A STEP FORWARD, I'LL DAMN WELL EDUCATE YOU.
OH, HUSH.
GET HER SOME CAFFEINE. COFFEE, MAYBE. COLD, HOT, DOESN'T MATTER.
IF SHE'S GOT A SACK OF FROZEN PEAS, BRING THAT.
TURN THE LIGHTS OFF ON THE WAY OUT.
JESSICA, RIGHT?
YOU'RE HAVING A MIGRAINE, JESSICA.
YOU'RE SAFE.
THINK OF WHAT YOU WANT MOST IN THE WORLD, YOUR HAPPIEST THOUGHTS.
I'M GOING TO JUST STROKE YOUR HAIR-- GENTLY, OKAY?
DON'T.
STOP.
...
DON'T STOP.

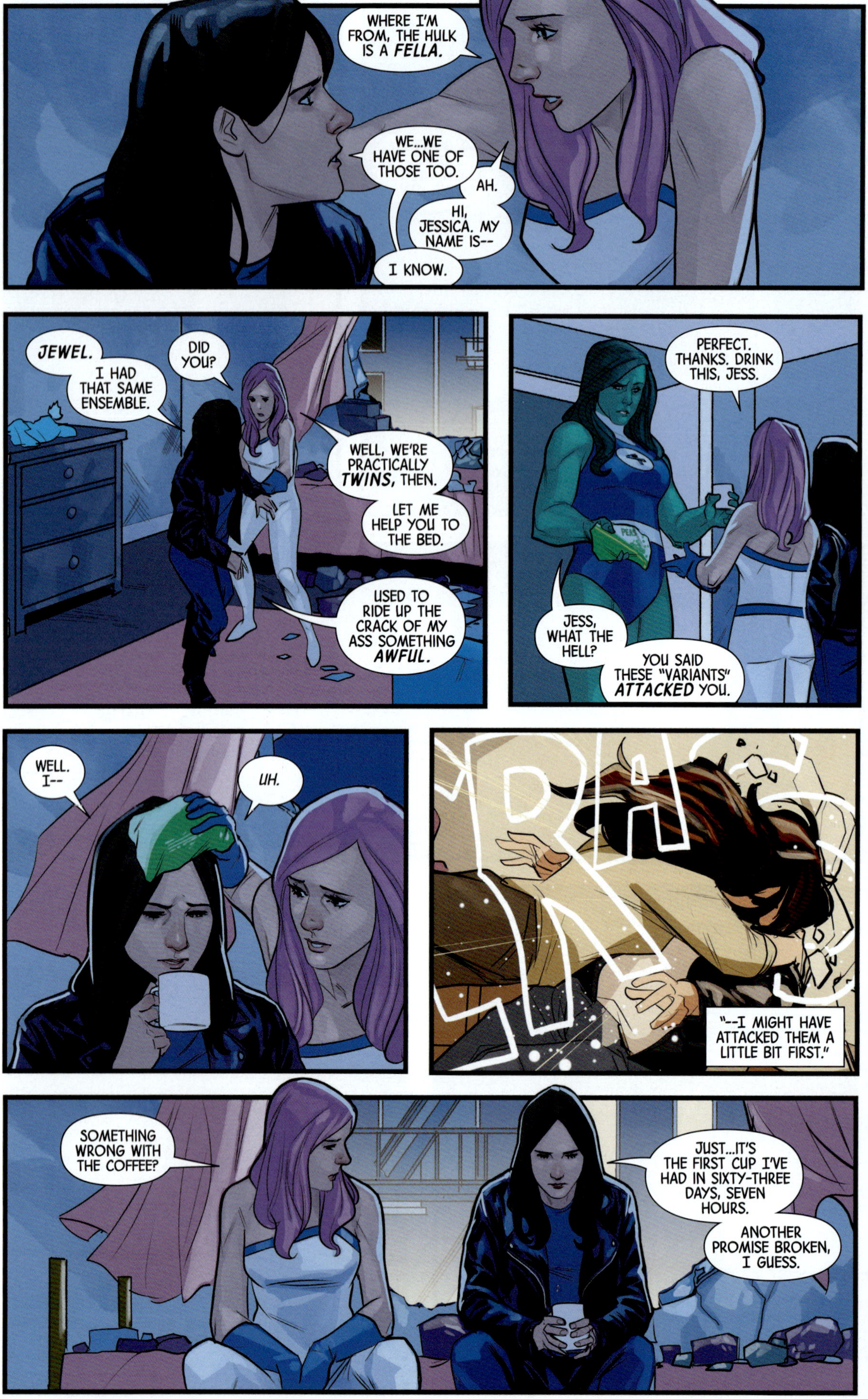

WHERE I'M FROM, THE HULK IS A *FELLA.*
WE...WE HAVE ONE OF THOSE TOO.
AH.
HI, JESSICA. MY NAME IS--
I KNOW.
JEWEL.
I HAD THAT SAME ENSEMBLE.
DID YOU?
WELL, WE'RE PRACTICALLY *TWINS,* THEN.
LET ME HELP YOU TO THE BED.
USED TO RIDE UP THE CRACK OF MY ASS SOMETHING *AWFUL.*
PERFECT. THANKS. DRINK THIS, JESS.
JESS, WHAT THE HELL?
YOU SAID THESE "VARIANTS" *ATTACKED* YOU.
WELL. I--
UH.
"--I MIGHT HAVE ATTACKED THEM A LITTLE BIT FIRST."
SOMETHING WRONG WITH THE COFFEE?
JUST...IT'S THE FIRST CUP I'VE HAD IN SIXTY-THREE DAYS, SEVEN HOURS.
ANOTHER PROMISE BROKEN, I GUESS.

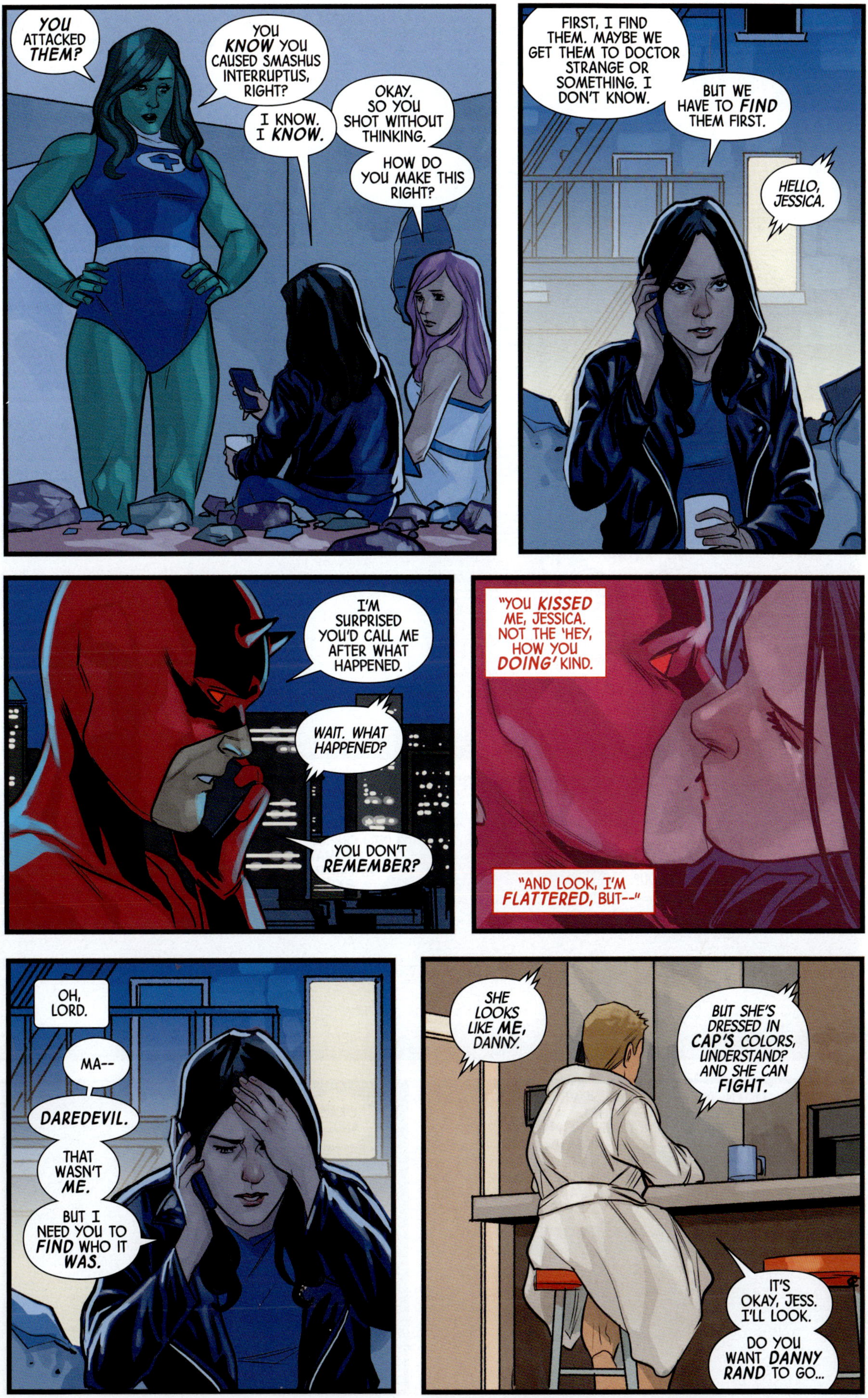
YOU ATTACKED THEM?
YOU KNOW YOU CAUSED SMASHUS INTERRUPTUS, RIGHT?
I KNOW. I KNOW.
OKAY. SO YOU SHOT WITHOUT THINKING.
HOW DO YOU MAKE THIS RIGHT?
FIRST, I FIND THEM. MAYBE WE GET THEM TO DOCTOR STRANGE OR SOMETHING. I DON'T KNOW.
BUT WE HAVE TO FIND THEM FIRST.
HELLO, JESSICA.
I'M SURPRISED YOU'D CALL ME AFTER WHAT HAPPENED.
WAIT. WHAT HAPPENED?
YOU DON'T REMEMBER?
"YOU KISSED ME, JESSICA. NOT THE 'HEY, HOW YOU DOING' KIND.
"AND LOOK, I'M FLATTERED, BUT--"
OH, LORD.
MA--
DAREDEVIL.
THAT WASN'T ME.
BUT I NEED YOU TO FIND WHO IT WAS.
SHE LOOKS LIKE ME, DANNY.
BUT SHE'S DRESSED IN CAP'S COLORS, UNDERSTAND? AND SHE CAN FIGHT.
IT'S OKAY, JESS. I'LL LOOK.
DO YOU WANT DANNY RAND TO GO...

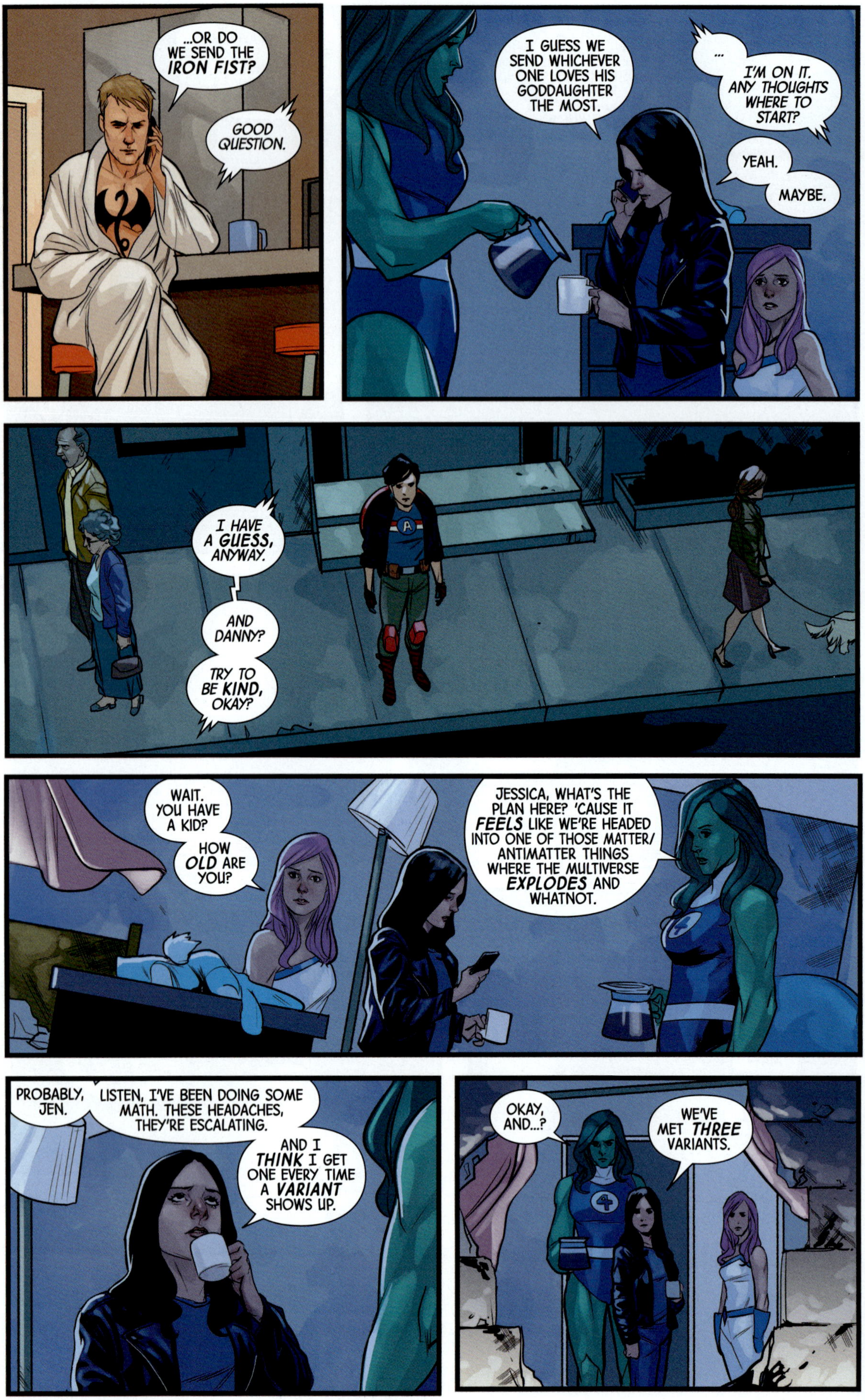
...OR DO WE SEND THE IRON FIST?
GOOD QUESTION.
I GUESS WE SEND WHICHEVER ONE LOVES HIS GODDAUGHTER THE MOST.
...
I'M ON IT. ANY THOUGHTS WHERE TO START?
YEAH.
MAYBE.
I HAVE A GUESS, ANYWAY.
AND DANNY?
TRY TO BE KIND, OKAY?
WAIT. YOU HAVE A KID?
HOW OLD ARE YOU?
JESSICA, WHAT'S THE PLAN HERE? 'CAUSE IT FEELS LIKE WE'RE HEADED INTO ONE OF THOSE MATTER/ ANTIMATTER THINGS WHERE THE MULTIVERSE EXPLODES AND WHATNOT.
PROBABLY, JEN.
LISTEN, I'VE BEEN DOING SOME MATH. THESE HEADACHES, THEY'RE ESCALATING.
AND I THINK I GET ONE EVERY TIME A VARIANT SHOWS UP.
OKAY, AND...?
WE'VE MET THREE VARIANTS.

"BUT I'VE HAD *FOUR* HEADACHES."

YOU.

YOU'RE NOT MY MATT, ARE YOU?

NO.

NO, MISS. I'M SORRY.

TRULY.

AND I--

--I DON'T BELONG HERE, DO I?

I KNOW YOU'RE WATCHING ME, WHOEVER YOU ARE.

ARE WE GOING TO HAVE A PROBLEM?

I HOPE NOT.

NO. WE'RE NOT GOING TO HAVE A PROBLEM.

WE HAD A MANSION LIKE THIS.

OUR AVENGERS DID, I MEAN.

THEN IT ALL JUST...

...WENT TO @&$% SOMEHOW.

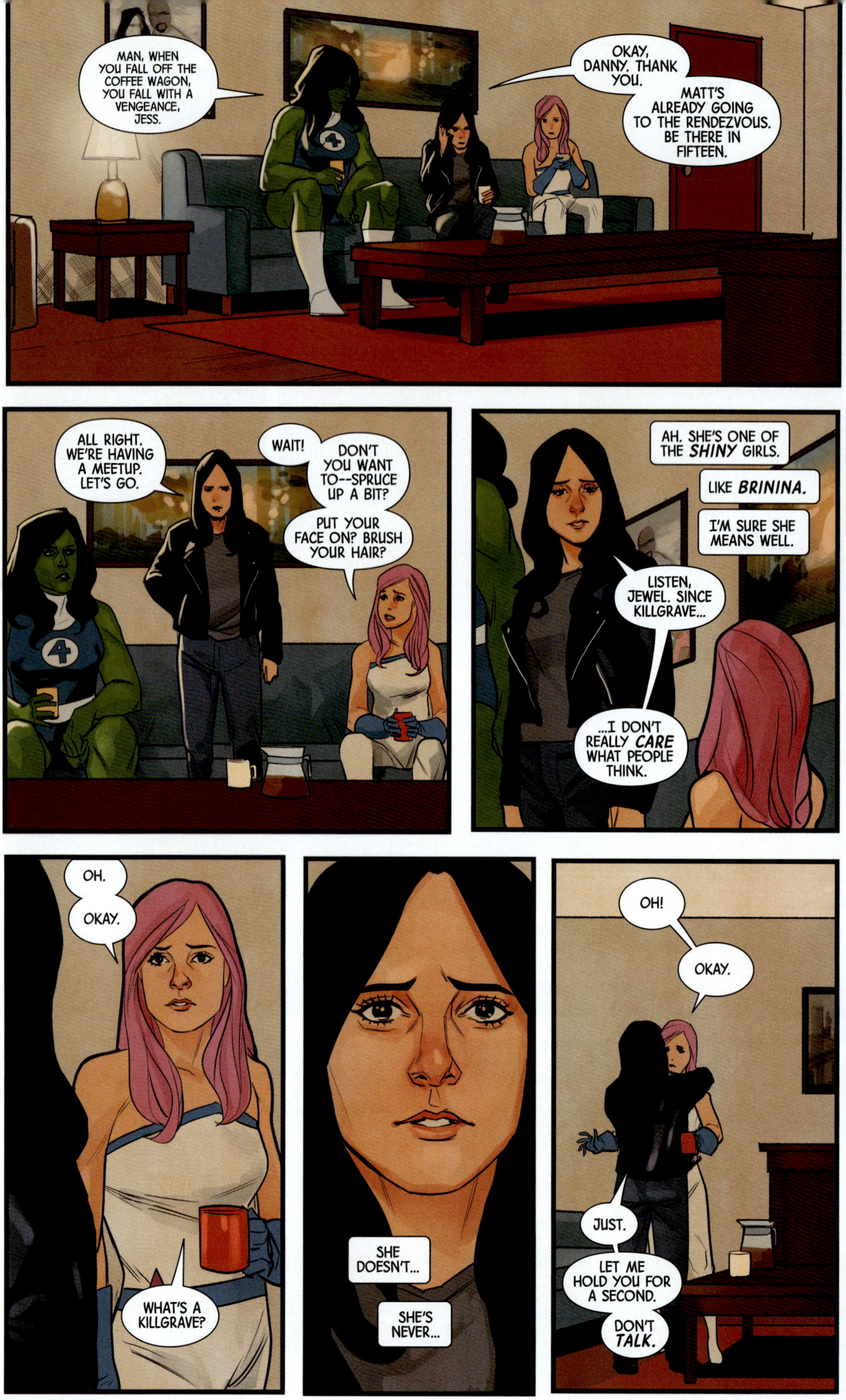
MAN, WHEN YOU FALL OFF THE COFFEE WAGON, YOU FALL WITH A VENGEANCE, JESS.
OKAY, DANNY. THANK YOU.
MATT'S ALREADY GOING TO THE RENDEZVOUS. BE THERE IN FIFTEEN.
ALL RIGHT. WE'RE HAVING A MEETUP. LET'S GO.
WAIT!
DON'T YOU WANT TO--SPRUCE UP A BIT?
PUT YOUR FACE ON? BRUSH YOUR HAIR?
AH. SHE'S ONE OF THE *SHINY* GIRLS.
LIKE *BRININA.*
I'M SURE SHE MEANS WELL.
LISTEN, JEWEL. SINCE KILLGRAVE...
...I DON'T REALLY *CARE* WHAT PEOPLE THINK.
OH.
OKAY.
WHAT'S A KILLGRAVE?
SHE DOESN'T...
SHE'S NEVER...
OH!
OKAY.
JUST.
LET ME HOLD YOU FOR A SECOND.
DON'T *TALK.*

SHE'S ME. OR AS NEAR AS, DAMMIT.
AND SHE'S NEVER HEARD OF THE PURPLE MAN.
OKAY. ONE PROMISE.
OKAY.
NO TALKING.
I'M GETTING THIS ONE HOME SAFE.
STOP LOOKING AT ME.
C'MON.
WHERE ARE WE GOING?
"WHERE ELSE?
"TO GET MORE COFFEE."
STOMPING GROUNDS
THOUGHT YOU WAS REAL SMART, DIDN'T YOU, RIO?
DIDN'T WANT TO PAY A PERFECTLY FAIR AMOUNT OF PROTECTION NO MORE, RIGHT?
SO YOU WENT AN' HIRED THAT BUTCH DAME TO SCARE MY BOYS.
BREAK MY LEG, EVEN!
SNACKS
HOT
EXTRAS
COCONUT MILK...50
WHIPPED CREAM...25
FLAVOR SHOT...50
SOY MILK...50
ESPRESSO SHOT...1.25
MORE

ONLY, SEE, NOBODY WELCHES ON HAMMERHEAD.
BUT YOU AREN'T MR. HAMM--
STOW THAT TALK, BEAN JOCKEY!
'CAUSE I BROUGHT A LITTLE MUSCLE OF MY OWN.
MEET BRUTO. THE STRONGMAN.
FROM THE CIRCUS OF CRIME, LITTLE MAN.
GEEZ.
THEM DANISH LOOK REAL GOOD, BOSS.
FORGET THE PASTRY, YOU CHUMP.
BASH SOME HEADS.
REMIND THESE MOPES WHO RUNS THIS BLOCK!
YEAH.
ABOUT THAT...
...I'M JUST ASKING.
WHO RUNS THIS BLOCK AGAIN?
I BELIEVE YOU ALREADY MET ONE OF MY COLLEAGUES HERE?

"YOU RUN THIS BLOCK. WE DON'T EVEN *LIVE* HERE!"

"PATHETIC. CAN I HAVE THEM DANISH, PLEASE?"

"AND THEM *COOKIES* TOO, THANKS."

"OKAY. THIS IS AWKWARD, BUT...WHAT DO WE *CALL* EACH OTHER?"

"CAP AND JEWEL, THOSE ARE EASY, BUT--"

"IT'S OKAY, JESSICA. IT'S YOUR REALITY, LOOKS LIKE. YOU CAN BE PRIME."

"MY CALL SIGN AT S.W.O.R.D. WAS OMEGA."

"OR CALL ME GROUCH GIRL."

"DOESN'T MATTER. WHO CARES?"

"MATT TOLD ME, OMEGA. THAT YOU WERE MARRIED TO YOUR DAREDEVIL."

"I'M SORRY FOR YOUR LOSS."

IT WAS STILT-WOMAN. CAN YOU BELIEVE IT?
FRICKING STILT-WOMAN.
ULTRON.
CONDORMAN.
I DON'T WANT TO TALK ABOUT THIS.
CAN THIS REALLY BE?
I'M SO, SO SORRY.
CAN I ACTUALLY BE IN A GROUP...
...WHERE MY SCREWED-UP LIFE IS THE LUCKY ONE?
THAT'S... THAT'S A LOT OF GRIEF FOR ONE LITTLE TABLE.
WE OUGHT TO CALL OURSELVES THE BLACK WIDOWS.
I'M AFRAID SOMEONE'S PARKED IN THAT SPOT ALREADY, JEWEL.
BUT I LIKE THE IDEA. WE'RE ALMOST SISTERS, RIGHT?
RIO! CHECK, PLEASE.
IT IS WEIRD, RIGHT?
THAT WE ALL LOST OUR LOVES LIKE THAT.
TO VIOLENCE.

EXCEPT THAT'S NOT ENTIRELY TRUE, PEP RALLY.
OUR HOST STILL HAS HER WARM BED.
KID TOO.
LUCKY HER.
SPEAKING OF WHICH, WHERE IS THE BIG MAN?
HE'S SAFE. I HAVE NO IDEA WHERE.
BUT HE'S SAFE.
YOU SENT HIM INTO HIDING?
BECAUSE OF US?
NO.
IT WAS SOMETHING ELSE.
I'M GOING TO THE LOBBY FOR A MINUTE, JUST TO GRAB SOME AIR. YOU TWO OKAY?
GO. BREATHE. WE GOT THIS, LUCAS.
AUNT MISTY TRIED TO PLAY A FIRE TYPE ON A CLOUD FACTION!
SHE LEFT HER BRAIN IN THE CATBOX!

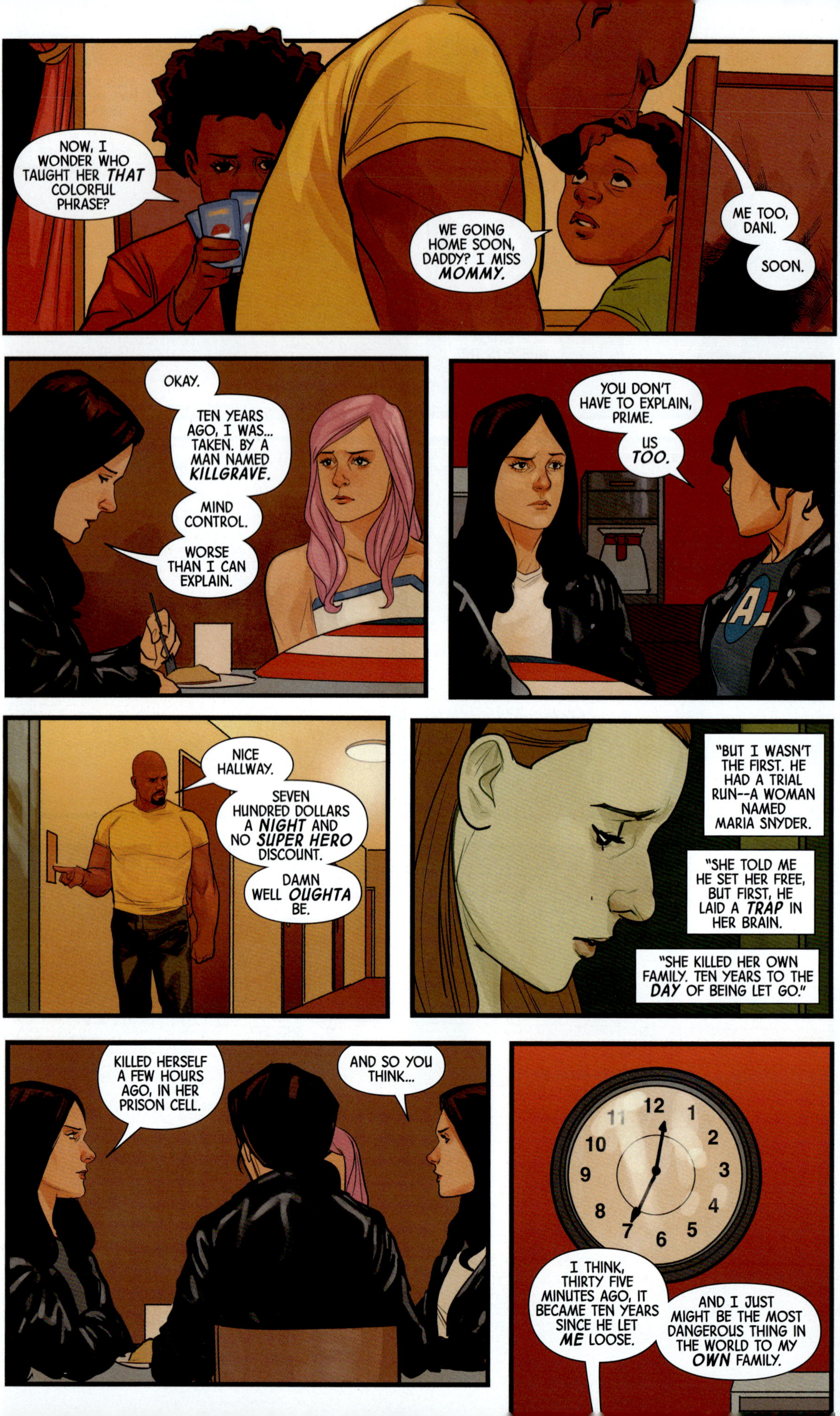
NOW, I WONDER WHO TAUGHT HER THAT COLORFUL PHRASE?
WE GOING HOME SOON, DADDY? I MISS MOMMY.
ME TOO, DANI.
SOON.
OKAY.
TEN YEARS AGO, I WAS... TAKEN. BY A MAN NAMED KILLGRAVE.
MIND CONTROL.
WORSE THAN I CAN EXPLAIN.
YOU DON'T HAVE TO EXPLAIN, PRIME.
US TOO.
NICE HALLWAY.
SEVEN HUNDRED DOLLARS A NIGHT AND NO SUPER HERO DISCOUNT.
DAMN WELL OUGHTA BE.
"BUT I WASN'T THE FIRST. HE HAD A TRIAL RUN--A WOMAN NAMED MARIA SNYDER.
"SHE TOLD ME HE SET HER FREE, BUT FIRST, HE LAID A TRAP IN HER BRAIN.
"SHE KILLED HER OWN FAMILY. TEN YEARS TO THE DAY OF BEING LET GO."
KILLED HERSELF A FEW HOURS AGO, IN HER PRISON CELL.
AND SO YOU THINK...
I THINK, THIRTY FIVE MINUTES AGO, IT BECAME TEN YEARS SINCE HE LET ME LOOSE.
AND I JUST MIGHT BE THE MOST DANGEROUS THING IN THE WORLD TO MY OWN FAMILY.

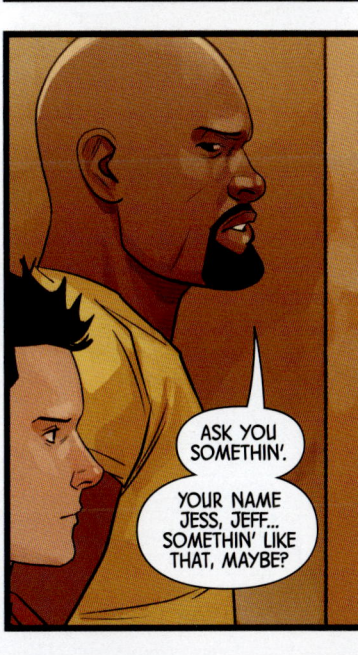

EVENIN'.

EVENIN'.

ASK YOU SOMETHIN'. YOUR NAME JESS, JEFF... SOMETHIN' LIKE THAT, MAYBE?

JESSE.

OKAY, JESSE. WE GONNA LET THE LITTLE OLD WHITE LADY GET OUT FIRST?

OKAY.

HATE TO MESS UP THIS NICE OL' ELEVATOR THOUGH. BRING IT.

BAM!

GUHH.

GNN.
POW!
STRONG. SO YOU'RE STRONG, IS THAT IT?
SHOW ME, LITTLE MAN.
WHACK!
HNNFFF.
KRASSH!!
DRIP COFFEE 2.29
DOUBLE ESPRESSO 2.79
OH, JESSICA. THAT'S--THAT'S AWFUL.
SO THAT'S WHY YOU HAD THE BIG GREEN GIRL--
YEAH. SHE'S MAKING SURE I DON'T KILL MY OWN HUSBAND AND DAUGHTER.

BUT SHE-HULK DOESN'T UNDERSTAND. SHE CAN'T *KNOW* WHAT KILLGRAVE DOES TO YOUR...YOUR *WIRING*.

SO I NEED YOU ALL TO PROMISE. IF I GO OVER, YOU'LL STOP ME.

EVEN IF THAT MEANS *STOP* STOP ME.

UNDERSTOOD, JESSICA.

I DON'T LIKE YOU, PRIME. I DON'T LIKE WHO YOU ARE, I DON'T LIKE WHAT YOU STILL HAVE.

BUT IF NECESSARY, I PROMISE--

"--I'LL TAKE YOU OUT *MYSELF*."

DAMMIT. LET ME *BEAT* ON YOU FOR A DAMN SECOND!

HAVE A NICE EVENING, LADIES. NO HURRY ON THE BILL.

THANKS.

I GOT THIS, LADIES.

EVERYTHING OKAY, JESSICA?

...

YEAH. JUST...

...IT'S JUST KIND OF A *LOT*.

Stomping Grounds

DON'T TRUST THEM

4 Coffees 20.00
1 Croiss   4.69

Total   4.69

I DON'T WANT TO DO THIS.
IT'S NOT ME, MAN.
I'M JUST THE BULLET.
YEAH?
WELL.
HOW SAD FOR YOU, FRIEND.
KRSSH!!
BECAUSE LUKE CAGE?
IS DAMN BULLETPROOF.
BAM!!

OH.
ALL RIGHT, LISTEN. WE'RE GONNA GET YOU TO A HOSPITAL. FIX YOU--FIX YOU UP.
NO.
BETTER THIS WAY.
LUKE.
REALLY WERE FRIENDS. SOMEWHERE.
IT'S COMING, LUKE.
COMING FOR HER
IT'S COMING FOR YOUR DAUGHTER
SORRY
SORR--
NO.
DANI.
DAAANNNNIIIIII!

MARVEL
THE VARIANTS
$3.99
4
SEP
APPROVED BY THE BREVOORT CODE AUTHORITY
VARIANTS ASSEMBLE!
noto

I THOUGHT OF THEM AS DUPLICATES. BUT THAT'S WRONG.
I THOUGHT THEY'D BE JUST...MORE OF *ME,* SOMEHOW.
BUT THAT'S NOT IT AT ALL.
THEY'RE MORE... DIVERGENT, I GUESS?
THEY'RE WHO I *COULD* HAVE BEEN.
FREAKING *CAP* HERE ACTUALLY LEADS HER WORLD'S *AVENGERS.*
PRIME, YOU OKAY?
AND *THIS* ONE, *JEWEL.*
SHE NEVER MET KILLGRAVE. NEVER HAD HER SPIRIT *FLAYED.*
KINDNESS RADIATES OFF HER.
AND IT BREAKS MY HEART A LITTLE.
SHE'S RIGHT, JESSICA. YOU LOOK SHOOK, SWEETIE.
AND THEN THERE'S *OMEGA.*
SHE DOESN'T LIKE ME. SHE DOESN'T *WANT* TO LIKE ME.
I KNOW HER. I *WAS* HER.
FOR A LONG, LONG TIME.
FOR CRIPES' SAKE. ARE WE HER AFFIRMATION CIRCLE NOW?

HERE. SINCE YOU'RE ALL FEELING SO BAD FOR THE ONLY ONE OF US WHO STILL HAS A FAMILY...
...LET'S SEE EXACTLY WHO IT IS WE'RE WEEPING FOR, OKAY?
"PRIME." YOU GOT A PICTURE OF YOUR FAMILY ON YOU?
YEAH. OF COURSE I DO. WHY?
GIVE IT. I JUST NEED IT FOR A SECOND.
DON'T LIKE WHERE THIS IS GOING.
TAKE A GOOD LOOK AT YOUR BLISS, SIS.
REALLY DRINK IT IN.
GNNAAAAAA!

WHACK
OH.
OH NO.
WHAT?
WHAT DID I JUST--?
MMFF.
GONNA THROW UP.
JESSICA.
LET HER GO, JEWEL.
GIVE HER ROOM.
THAT WAS MEAN.
WAS IT?
BETTER SHE KNOWS NOW, I SHOULD THINK.
BETTER A PHOTO THAN HER FAMILY.
OHMY GODOHMY GOD.
DON'T MOVE. DON'T TALK.
I KNOW WHAT THIS IS. I KNOW WHAT I'M HAVING.
BUT I CAN'T STOP IT. CAN'T EVEN SLOW IT DOWN.

IT'S A BONE-DEEP, FULL-ON PANIC ATTACK.
GET OFF ME.
WHAM!!
YOU PICKED A BAD DAY.
NO.
YOU PICKED THE WORST DAY!
I NEED CONTROL. I NEED TO CALM DOWN.
BUT YOU KNOW WHAT?
KRRSSHH!!
MAYBE I JUST DON'T FEEL LIKE IT AT THE MOMENT.

DAMMIT, JESSICA, GET A GRIP.
I'M TRYING TO SAVE YOU, YOU COMPLETE D-BAG!
WAIT. YOU'RE ONE OF THEM. YOU'RE ME.
KNIGHTRESS.
YEAH, YEAH. I'M YOU WITHOUT ALL THE POINTLESS RAGE.
HELP ME UP, J-HULK.
DIDN'T YOU GET MY NOTE?
"I WAS DRESSED AS A WAITRESS? I STAND BY THAT MESSAGE, BY THE WAY."
CHK 20785
4 Coffees 20.00
1 Croiss 4.69
Total
DON'T TRUST THEM
I DON'T KNOW WHAT'S HAPPENING.
BELIEVE ME, THAT'S PAINFULLY OBVIOUS.
YOUR HUBS WAS A NEW AVENGER, RIGHT?
WE NEED TO CALL HIM. NOW.
I SENT HIM INTO HIDING. TO KEEP THEM SAFE.
SUPER NOBLE, I'M SURE. BUT HE'S GOT SOMETHING WE NEED.
AND WHAT IS THAT, EXACTLY?
WOLVERINE ON SPEED DIAL.
NOW BE A PAL AND HAND ME SOME PAPER TOWELS, FOR GOD'S SAKE. I'VE GOT TOILET HEAD.
Lucas Cage (616)

OKAY, TEAM OF FREAKS?
MEET KNIGHTRESS.
KNIGHTRESS? TEAM OF FREAKS.
ENOUGH COFFEE.
WE'RE OUT OF HERE, LADIES.
JESSICA, WHAT'S HAPPENING?
WE'RE GOING TO HAVE A SEANCE.
AND WE'RE GONNA MESS SOMEONE ALL THE WAY UP.
WHO'S IN?
RISKY DOING THIS AT HOME... BUT WE CAN'T BE INTERRUPTED.
PLEASE LET HER BE TELLING THE TRUTH.
WHY ARE WE ON YOUR ROOF, JESSICA? WOULDN'T YOU BE MORE COMFORTABLE INSIDE?
THERE'S FIVE ANGRY MEs IN THIS EQUATION, AND YOU ALREADY BLEW OUT MY DAUGHTER'S BEDROOM WALL, JEWEL.
LET'S PRETEND WE'RE CAMPING.
YOU SURE ABOUT THIS?
NO, JESSICA.
NOT EVEN REMOTELY.
OKAY.
HOW DO WE DO IT, THEN?
YOU KNOW HOW.
YOU'VE FOUGHT HIS MEMORY EVERY DAY FOR TEN YEARS.
STOP FIGHTING.
INVITE HIM IN, JESSICA.
ALL RIGHT. HEY, YOU MISERABLE PURPLE BASTARD...
WELCOME HOME.

I BROUGHT YOU A PILLOW FROM YOUR BEDROOM, JESSICA.
WE GOT YOU.
DANI IS GONNA BE FINE, OKAY?
...
THANK YOU, JEWEL. JUST--
--THANK YOU.
I'M SCARED. I SAID IT, ALL RIGHT?
I'M SCARED.
MIGHTY *CONVENIENT* THAT A PLAYER WE DON'T *KNOW* SHOWS UP WITH A PLAN *TONIGHT.*
LOOK, "OMEGA." IF WE DON'T KILL EACH OTHER, WE CAN BOUNCE ACCUSATIONS ALL *OVER* THE PLACE, ALL RIGHT?
AFTER THE EXORCISM.
WELL, I DON'T LIKE *THAT* WORDING.
STAND *DOWN,* SOLDIERS.
WE AGREED TO HELP.
FORM A PERIMETER, FACING OUT. YOU HEARD WHAT HER HUSBAND SAID.
THERE COULD BE *MORE* OUT THERE.
YOU'RE RIGHT.
TAKE CARE, PRIME. YOU CAN *DO* THIS.
TRY TO THINK OF SOMETHING THAT MAKES YOU *STRONG.*
YEAH.
I GOT THE POWER.

Panel 1:
THEY'RE SCARED TOO.
BECAUSE OF WHAT *LUKE* SAID FIFTEEN MINUTES AGO.
YEAH. A GUY VERSION OF *YOU*, JESS.
HE *FOUND* US SOMEHOW.

Panel 2:
I SORTA PUSHED HIM OUT THE WINDOW.
THEN HE CAUGHT *FIRE*.
IS SHE--?
DANI'S OKAY. SHE'S OKAY.

Panel 3:
SHE ALSO HAD A COUPLE ANGELS ON HER SHOULDER.
JESS? STILL THERE?
... I WAS AFRAID YOU DIDN'T BELIEVE ME.

Panel 4:
BABY.
I ALWAYS BELIEVE YOU.
DON'T YOU KNOW THAT BY NOW?

Panel 5:
I DO. IT'S JUST...
I JUST FEEL LUCKY, SOMETIMES. I MARRIED INTO MAGIC.
I NEED YOU TO FIND A DARKER HOLE, IF YOU CAN.

Panel 6:
IT'S OKAY, JESS.
I HAVE A *RIDE*.

AND NOW ANYONE COULD BE OUT THERE, WORSE VERSIONS OF ME.

AND I'M NOT AT ALL SURE IT'S ANGELS LOOKING OUT FOR ME THIS TIME.

I'M HERE, KILLGRAVE.

LET'S CHAT.

HELLO, PET.

SEEM FAMILIAR?

DAMMIT.

THAT SAME CREEPING FEAR UP MY SPINE.

AW, DON'T BE CROSS, LET'S NOT BE CROSS.

GET OFF ME. GET OFF.

NOW, NOW, HONEY SWEET.

YOU CALLED ME, REMEMBER?

WHY PLAY HARD TO GET NOW?

THAT LOATHSOME SACK OF SNAILS AND RAW MEAT.

DON'T SHOW HIM, JESSICA.

DON'T SHOW THAT YOU'RE FULL *UP* ON TERROR.

YOU PUT A TIME BOMB IN ME.

LIKE THE ONE YOU PUT IN MARIA SNYDER.

BEFORE SHE *KILLED* HERSELF IN HER CRAPPY JAIL CELL.

OLD *NEWS*, PET. WHAT WAS THAT, TWO DAYS AGO?

I'D RATHER TALK ABOUT *US*.

STILL HAVEN'T FULLY LOST YOUR *BABY* WEIGHT, I SEE.

YOU WANT ME TO KILL MY OWN FAMILY.

WHY?

YOU ALREADY *TOOK* EVERYTHING FROM ME.

→SIGH← AFTER ALL THIS TIME. ALL THIS *INTIMACY*.

YOU STILL DON'T UNDERSTAND ME AT ALL, DO YOU, PET?

DO YOU KNOW WHY I CHOSE YOU?

WHY I *KEPT* YOU, YOU WORTHLESS LITTLE RODENT?

WAIT.

DID I SAY YOU COULD SMILE?

WHY ARE YOU *SMILING*, FILTH?

BECAUSE I CALLED A FRIEND OF A FRIEND, KILLGRAVE. ON THE LONG-DISTANCE LINE FROM *KRAKOA*.

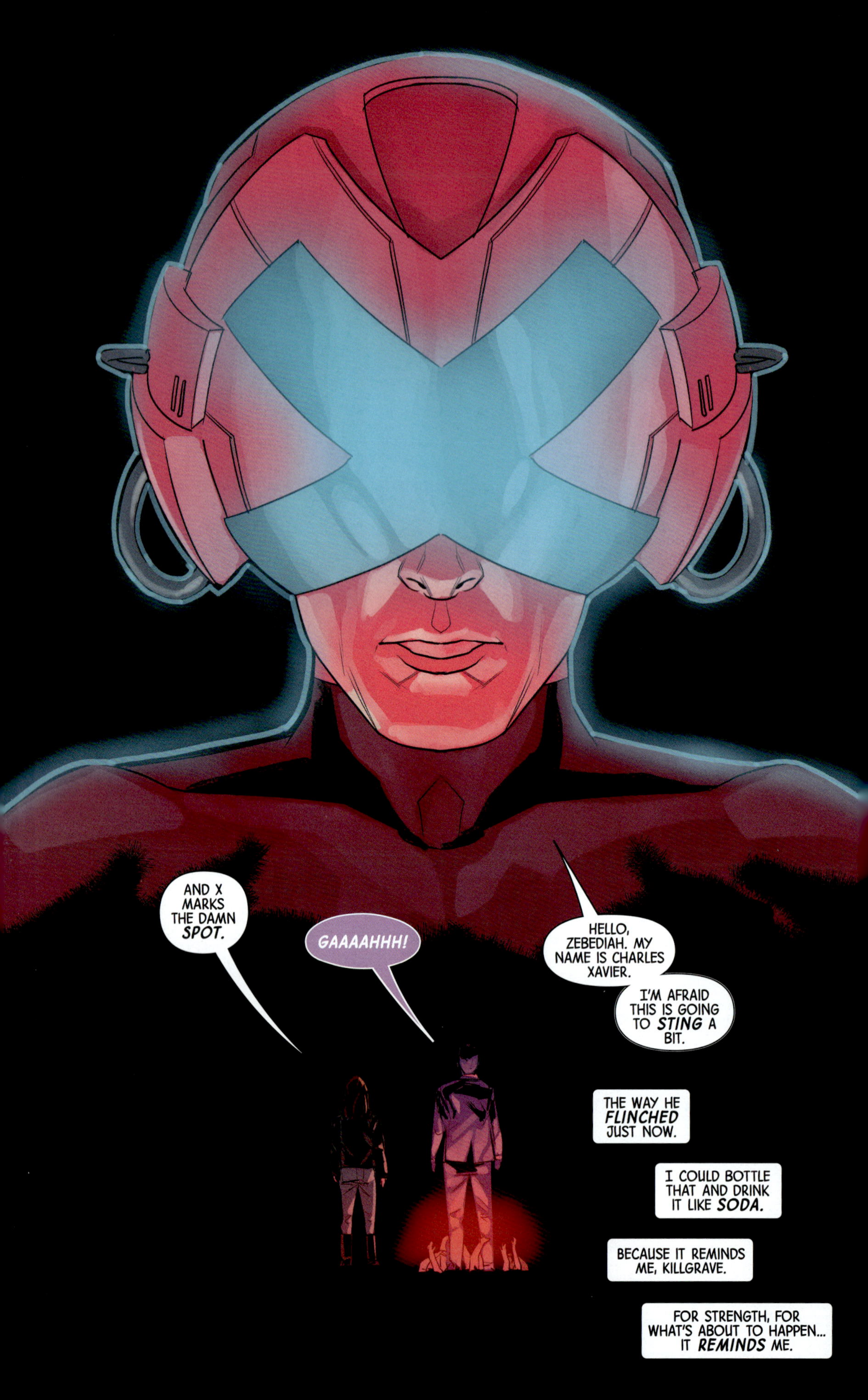
AND X MARKS THE DAMN SPOT.
GAAAAHHH!
HELLO, ZEBEDIAH. MY NAME IS CHARLES XAVIER.
I'M AFRAID THIS IS GOING TO STING A BIT.
THE WAY HE FLINCHED JUST NOW.
I COULD BOTTLE THAT AND DRINK IT LIKE SODA.
BECAUSE IT REMINDS ME, KILLGRAVE.
FOR STRENGTH, FOR WHAT'S ABOUT TO HAPPEN... IT REMINDS ME.

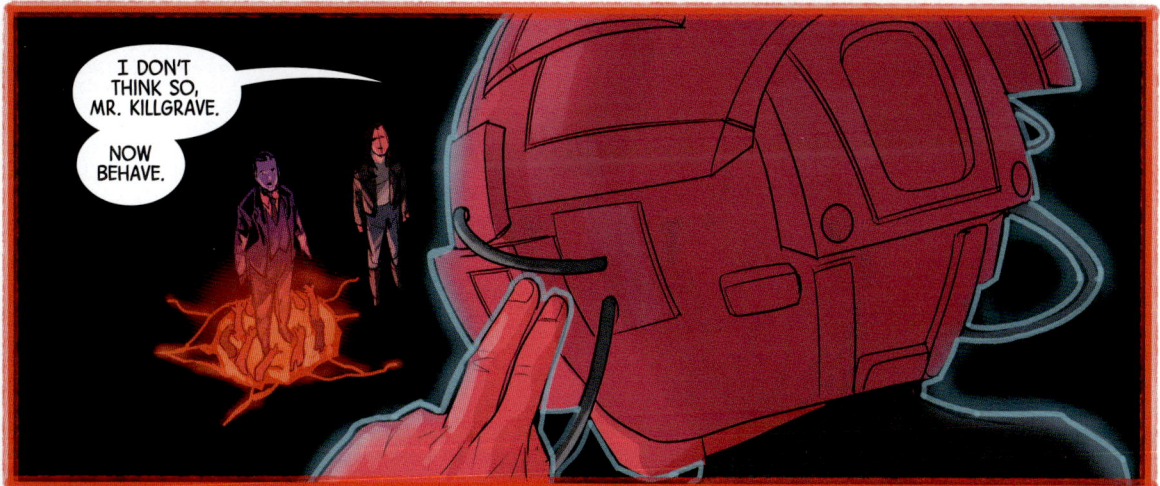

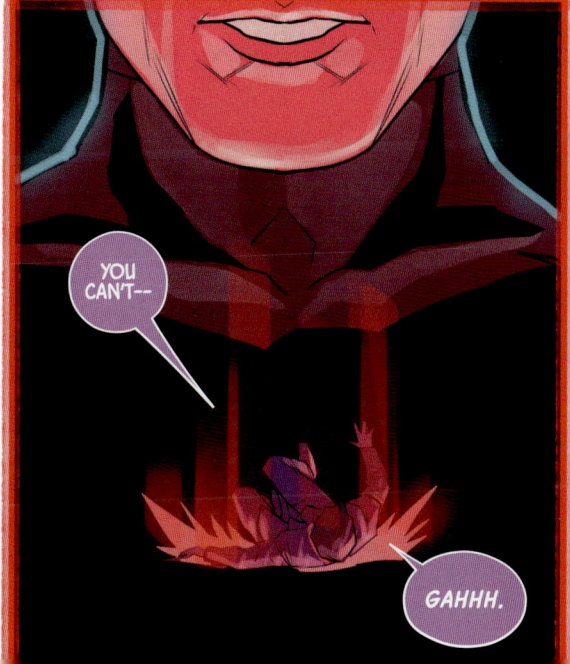

THAT AT YOUR HEART, AT YOUR VERY CORE...

...YOU ARE NOTHING BUT A DAMP LITTLE COWARD.

YOU... YOU SET A TRAP? FOR ME?

YOU INSIGNIFICANT TRAMPOLINE.

YOU DISOBEDIENT FUNGUS.

I'LL MAKE YOU SUFFER LIKE NO ONE ELSE HAS!

I DON'T THINK SO, MR. KILLGRAVE.

NOW BEHAVE.

NO. NO. WHAT ARE YOU DOING?

YOU CAN'T--

GAHHH.

OH, DO BE QUIET, WON'T YOU?
GUHHHH
STOP.
NO. DON'T.
MERCY!
"MERCY"?
I CAN SEE JESSICA'S MEMORIES, ZEBEDIAH.
I DON'T THINK MERCY IS QUITE IN ORDER, DO YOU?
KRAK
AARRGHHHH!
AND I MUST SAY, THE DECOR IN HERE IS UNPRODUCTIVE TO A HEALING ENVIRONMENT.
DO YOU HAVE A FAVORITE FLOWER, JESSICA?
ROSES.
PINK ROSES. MORNING BLUSH.
AS GIRLY AS YOU CAN MAKE THEM.
PINK ROSES IT SHALL BE, THEN.
NO.
NOOOOOOO!
EVERY VICTIM'S DREAM.
TO SEE THEIR ABUSER CRAWL.

I COULD GET USED TO IT, I WON'T LIE.
WHAT WAS IT YOU WERE GOING TO SAY, KILLGRAVE?
WHY ME?
...
BECAUSE YOU WERE STRONG.
TRY AGAIN, CALIFORNIA RAISIN.
AHHNNN.
BECAUSE YOU WERE HAPPY, ALL RIGHT?
IT'S BECAUSE YOU WERE HAPPY.
AND YOU COULDN'T STAND THAT.
...
YOU'RE PATHETIC.
THROW HIM OUT OF MY BRAIN, PROFESSOR. BURN HIM OUT, IF NECESSARY.
MS. JONES-CAGE.
I DON'T THINK YOU UNDERSTAND WHAT'S HAPPENING HERE.
WE...WE COULD HAVE BEEN BROTHERS. GODS.
JOIN ME. WE COULD RULE EVERYTHING.
NO.
I HAVE THREE QUESTIONS FOR YOU, MR. KILLGRAVE.
ANSWER THEM TRUTHFULLY.

WHAT WAS THE NAME OF YOUR FIRST PET?

WHAT WAS YOUR FAVORITE NOVEL AT AGE 15?

WHO WAS YOUR FIRST HIGH SCHOOL CRUSH?

QUICKLY NOW.

TERRY. PLANET TERRY.

PRIDE AND PREJUDICE.

PETER PARKER.

DAMN YOU.

WHOSE ANSWERS ARE THOSE, JESSICA?

MINE. THOSE ARE *MY* ANSWERS.

HOW...?

THE "TIME BOMB" IS REAL, JESSICA. HE PLANTED IT TEN YEARS AGO.

BUT THERE IS NO PART OF HIM IN YOUR MIND, NOT EVEN AN ELECTRON'S WORTH.

HE ISN'T DOING ANY OF THIS.

HE'S TOLD *YOU* TO PULL THAT TRIGGER.

MY GOD. I WOULD HAVE...

LUKE AND *DANI.*

WHAT DO I *DO?*

I'M AFRAID THAT'S THE DIFFICULT PART.

YOU HAVE TO *FORGIVE* HIM.

NO.

ANYTHING ELSE.

YOU MUST UNDERSTAND, JESSICA. HE ISN'T ME.
EVEN IF HE WEREN'T IN A COMA IN THE OUTSIDE WORLD, HE HAS NO CONNECTION TO YOU, BUT THIS.
HE WILL NEVER HEAR YOUR FORGIVENESS.
HE ONLY KNOWS WHAT YOU KNOW, ONLY SUSPECTS WHAT YOU DO.
BECAUSE HE IS YOU, JESSICA.
FORGIVE HIM, FORGIVE YOURSELF.
AND WALK AWAY IN PEACE.
NEVER.
WAKE ME UP, CHARLES.
LET ME GO HOME.

MOISTURE ON MY FACE.

AM I CRYING?

NO. IT'S STARTED RAINING. AND MY MIND IS *CLEAR*, THANK GOD.

NO MORE TEARS. NO MORE *HIDING*.

MISSION ACCOMPLISHED, SOLDIER?

FIXIN' TO BE, CAP.

THE VARIANT. SHE CALLED MY DAUGHTER OUT BY *NAME*.

I NEVER *SAID* HER NAME.

SHE BROKE IN. THE OTHERS TOOK THE DOOR.

SHE BROKE RIGHT INTO DANI'S *BEDROOM*.

JEWEL.

DID YOU COME HERE TO STEAL MY DAUGHTER?

BUSTED.

YOU MAD?

"JEWEL. I THOUGHT YOU WERE THE BEST OF ME."

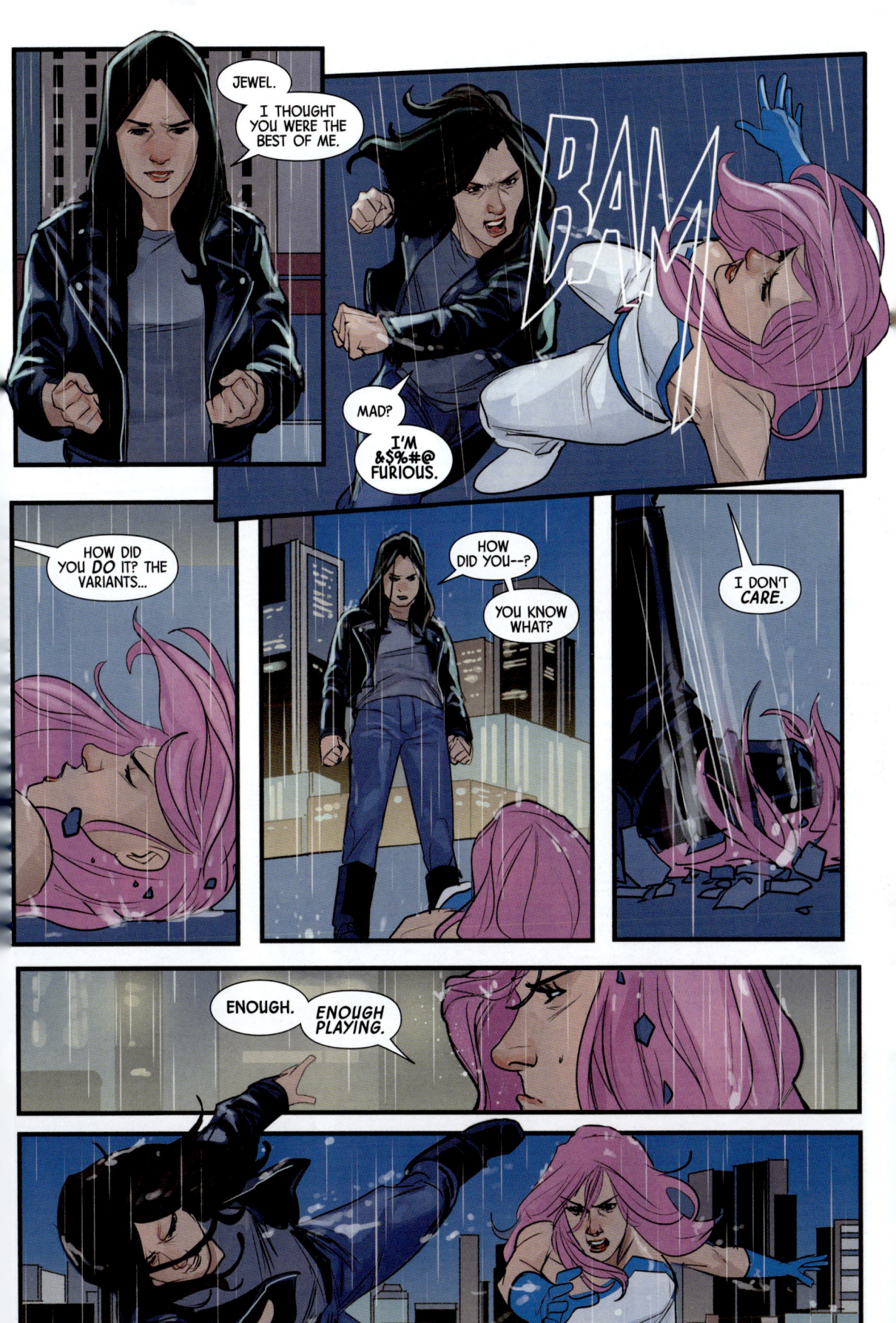

BAM

"MAD? I'M &$%#@ FURIOUS."

"HOW DID YOU *DO* IT? THE VARIANTS..."

"HOW DID YOU--?"

"YOU KNOW WHAT?"

"I DON'T *CARE*."

"ENOUGH. *ENOUGH PLAYING*."

Panel 1:
WHY DO YOU MAKE ME DO THIS?
I DON'T EVEN *LIKE* FIGHTING.
SO... YOU MAKE... *OTHERS*...DO YOUR KILLING?

Panel 2:
YES. BUT NOT *THIS* TIME.
NOT *THIS* TIME.

Panel 3:
GUHHN!
SSSHHKKUNGG!

Panel 4:
I'M AFRAID WE CAN'T ALLOW THAT, LADY.
YOU OWE US SOME *ANSWERS*.
STAND *DOWN*.
OR YOU COULD RESIST. BY ALL MEANS, *RESIST*.

OKAY.
MAYBE BEING PART OF A TEAM ISN'T THE WORST THING EVER.

Panel 5:
OH MY.
WELL, JESSICA.
I'M AFRAID THIS IS GOING TO *HURT*.
UH-OH.

OH GOD. THE MIGRAINE. IT'S BACK.
A HUNDRED TIMES WORSE.
THIS IS YOUR FAULT, JESSICA.
FOR BEING SO SELFISH.
VARIANTS?
ASSEMBLE.

5

THE MIGRAINES.
THEY HAPPEN EVERY... EVERY TIME A VARIANT COMES HERE.
TO MY WORLD.
AND OH HELL. THIS IS THE WORST ONE.
JESSICA. JESSICA.
I'M GONNA NEED YOU TO STAND UP, SOLDIER.
NOT GONNA LIE.
THE ODDS AREN'T GOOD.
YEAH.
WHEN ARE THEY EVER?
WORK, LEGS. STAND UP. DON'T YOU DARE TREMBLE UNDER ME.
THESE "VARIANTS," AT LEAST, SEEM TO BE ON MY TEAM.
WE PLAY THE CARDS WE'RE DEALT.
YOUR WORLD OR ANY WORLD...
...THAT'S ALL YOU GET.
I'VE BEEN FOLLOWING HER.
SHE'S LEFT A TRAIL OF GRIEF ALL OVER THE MULTIVERSE.
NEVER SAW HER FACE-TO-FACE UNTIL NOW.
GRIEF.

THE VARIANTS
FACE FRONT, TRUE BELIEVER...

JESSICA PRIME

CAPTAIN JESSICA

OMEGA

KNIGHTRESS

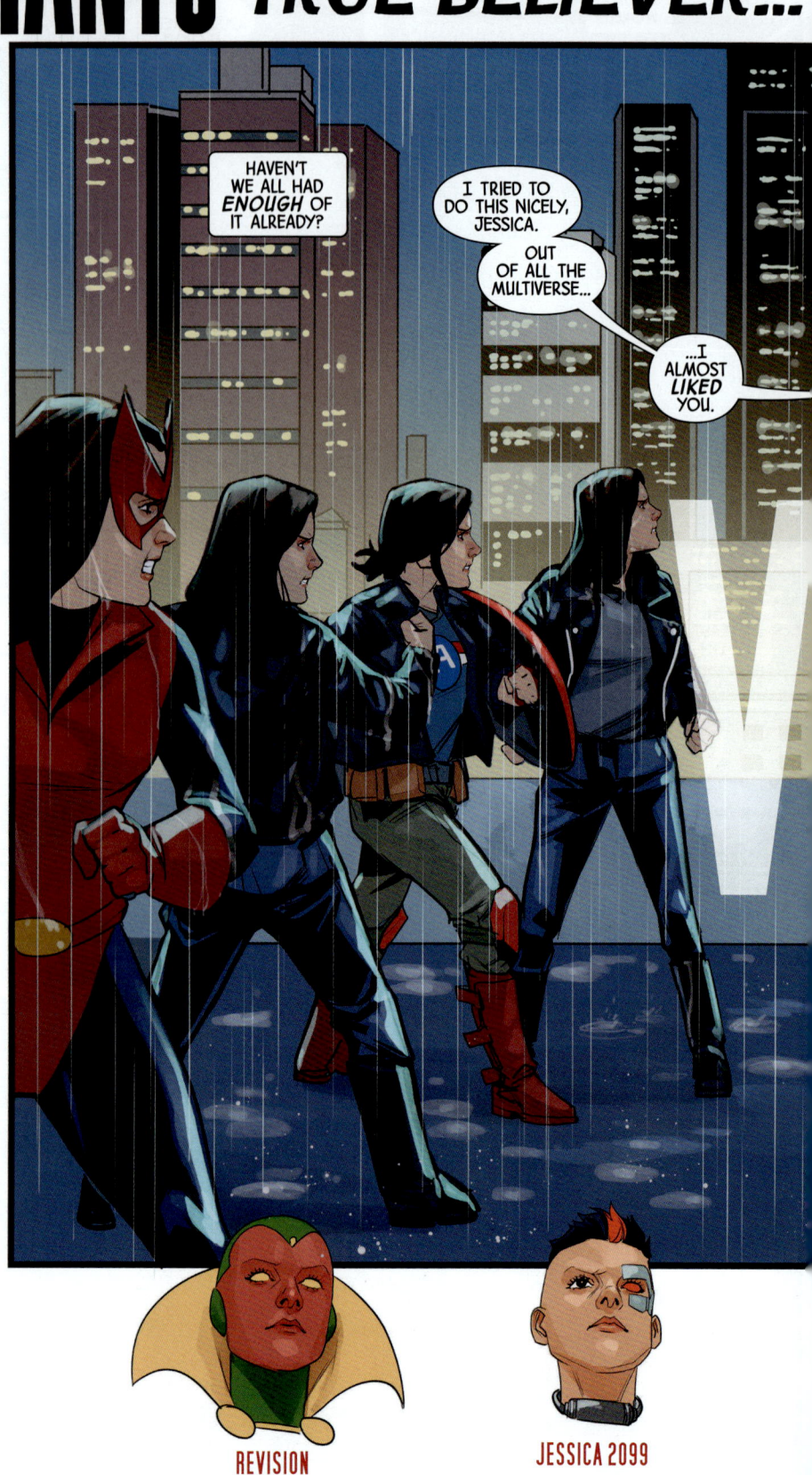

REVISION

JESSICA 2099

"HAVEN'T WE ALL HAD *ENOUGH* OF IT ALREADY?"

"I TRIED TO DO THIS NICELY, JESSICA. OUT OF ALL THE MULTIVERSE..."

"...I ALMOST *LIKED* YOU."

IT'S THE BATTLE YOU'VE BEEN WAITING FOR:

JEWEL

MOURNING BLUSH

SIGIL

POWER-WOMAN

ULTRA-JESS

ALIAS JESSI JAMES

THE VARIANTS

LIKED ME SO MUCH YOU BROUGHT A PLATOON.
I SAID "LIKED."
I DIDN'T SAY "TRUSTED."
PRIME.
EITHER LEAD THE CHARGE OR GET OUT OF THE WAY.
WHAT?
NO, DAMMIT.
WHAT DO YOU THINK THIS IS, THE CONTEST OF CHAMPIONS?
THIS IS MY DAMN HOUSE.
I'M NOT FIGHTING THEM.
I'M NOT FIGHTING ANYONE.
YOU.
YOU BROUGHT THEM ALL HERE.
WHAT IS IT EXACTLY THAT YOU WANT FROM ME?
COME ON. TELL ME.
YOU'RE DYING TO. I CAN SEE IT.

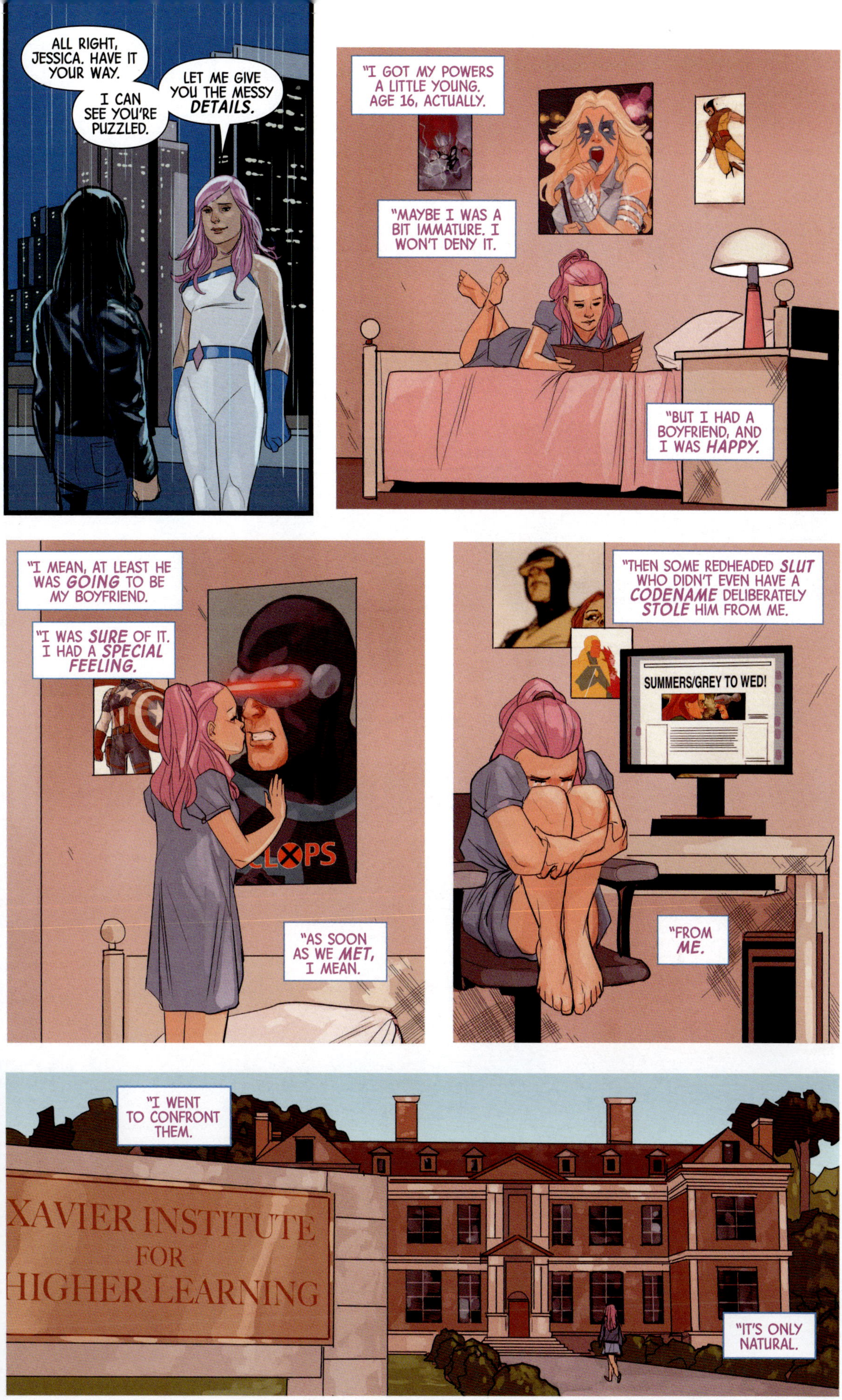
ALL RIGHT, JESSICA. HAVE IT YOUR WAY.
I CAN SEE YOU'RE PUZZLED.
LET ME GIVE YOU THE MESSY DETAILS.
"I GOT MY POWERS A LITTLE YOUNG. AGE 16, ACTUALLY.
"MAYBE I WAS A BIT IMMATURE. I WON'T DENY IT.
"BUT I HAD A BOYFRIEND, AND I WAS HAPPY.
"I MEAN, AT LEAST HE WAS GOING TO BE MY BOYFRIEND.
"I WAS SURE OF IT. I HAD A SPECIAL FEELING.
CLOPS
"AS SOON AS WE MET, I MEAN.
"THEN SOME REDHEADED SLUT WHO DIDN'T EVEN HAVE A CODENAME DELIBERATELY STOLE HIM FROM ME.
SUMMERS/GREY TO WED!
"FROM ME.
"I WENT TO CONFRONT THEM.
XAVIER INSTITUTE FOR HIGHER LEARNING
"IT'S ONLY NATURAL.

"I ADMIT IT.

"I LOST MY TEMPER."

GOOD GOD IN HEAVEN.
YOU'RE TELLING ME... COLOSSUS, PHOENIX...
I COULDN'T TAKE EITHER ONE OF THEM ON MY BEST DAY.
HOW DID YOU EVEN...?
OH, JESSICA, JESSICA. YOU'RE PRECIOUS.
YOU THINK I HAVE YOUR POWERS?
NO, DEAR.
"THEY'RE MORE LIKE ROGUE'S.
"WHICH I DISCOVERED WHEN I BASHED HER SILLY FACE IN.
"IT WAS MY COMING OF AGE, JESSICA.
"THE DAY I BECAME A WOMAN.
XAVIER INSTITUTE FOR HIGHER LEARNING
"THE DAY I FIRST SHAMPOOED A HERO'S BLOOD OUT OF MY HAIR."
IT'S TRUE. THEY WERE MY FRIENDS.
THEN THEY WERE JUST...
...GONE.

THAT'S THE SICKEST THING I'VE EVER HEARD.
I'M JUST GETTING STARTED.
SEE, I SEARCHED FOR THAT SPECIAL FEELING. ALL OVER MY WORLD.
AVENGERS. DEFENDERS. NO CHEMISTRY.
"I'D TAKE THEIR STRENGTH. TAKE THEIR GIFTS. LEAVE THEM HELPLESS.
"BUT AFTER A FEW DAYS OF GLORY, THEY'D GO BACK TO THEIR OWNERS.
"UNTIL I MET A UNIQUE PRESENCE."
CAN YOU GUESS WHO HE WAS?
STRANGE.
YOU TRIED TO MARRY DOCTOR STRANGE?
OH, GOOD LORD, NO. NOT HUSBAND MATERIAL.
THAT GOATEE!
BUT I DID PULL THIS OFF HIS CORPSE.
JEWEL. WHATEVER YOUR NAME IS.
DID YOU... DO THIS THING TO OUR HUSBANDS?
IS THAT--?

THAT'S HOW THEY DIED, YES. I SIPHONED THEM WHILE THEY WERE IN COMBAT.
THEIR REJECTIONS WERE RUDE.
WHAT CHOICE DID I HAVE?
WIDOWS. BROKEN HEARTS THAT NEVER QUITE HEAL.
BECAUSE SOME TWISTED FOAL IS LOOKING FOR HER SOULMATE.
IT STOPS HERE.
EVIL LIKE THIS... IT CAN'T BE LEFT ALIVE.
IT FESTERS. IT INFECTS EVERYTHING AND EVERYONE.
AND THE JUSTICE BAND OF JESSICAS BEHIND ME?
THEY HAVE LOVED ONES ON THE LINE TOO.
IF YOU REFUSE MY KIND OFFER.
JESSICA JONES.
WILL YOU SWITCH LIVES WITH ME?
LUCAS... HE WOULD NEVER...
I'M YOUNGER.
I'M PRETTIER.
AND FRANKLY, I'M A BIT OF A LIBERTINE.
HE'LL ADJUST.

SHE'S NOT ANSWERING HER PHONE.
SOMETHING'S WRONG.
WE'LL TAKE CARE OF DANI, LUKE. GO GET YOUR WIFE.
BUT, MISTY...I MEAN, IF IT'S BAD. IF WE DON'T COME BACK...
YOU HEARD ME. ON BOTH COUNTS.
TELL DANI I LOVE HER. DON'T WAKE HER UP.
BUT TELL HER.
EVERY DAY.
GO TAKE CARE OF BUSINESS.
YEAH.
THAT'S KIND OF WHAT I'M GOOD AT.
WELL, LOOKEE HERE.
TURNS OUT I HAVE A TEMPER TOO.
OOOOFF.
BAM!
THE ANSWER IS "NO."
YOU STINKING TRASH.

I DISTINCTLY HEARD HER SAY "NO FIGHTING."
WE'RE BADLY OUTNUMBERED. AND *THESE* VARIANTS ARE JUST FIGHTING SO THEY DON'T LOSE *THEIR* LOVED ONES.
AYE OR NAY.
THEY BENT THE KNEE TO JEWEL, KNOWING WHAT SHE DID TO OUR FAMILIES. WHAT SHE'LL DO TO THE *KID*.
WE SEND THEM HOME *BLOODY*.
COPY THAT.
I ADMIRE THE *SPUNK*.
SHE...SHE REALLY *IS* CAPTAIN AMERICA, *HUH?*
GIVE PRIME COVER.
LET'S *AVENGER* THESE $#@%&#@.
YOU KNOW, THE MOMENT I SAW LUCAS...
...I GOT THAT SPECIAL FEELING.
I'M GOING TO DRAIN HIM. JUST A BIT. EVERY DAY.
I THINK HE'LL GROW TO LOVE IT. WHAT DO YOU THINK, JESSICA?

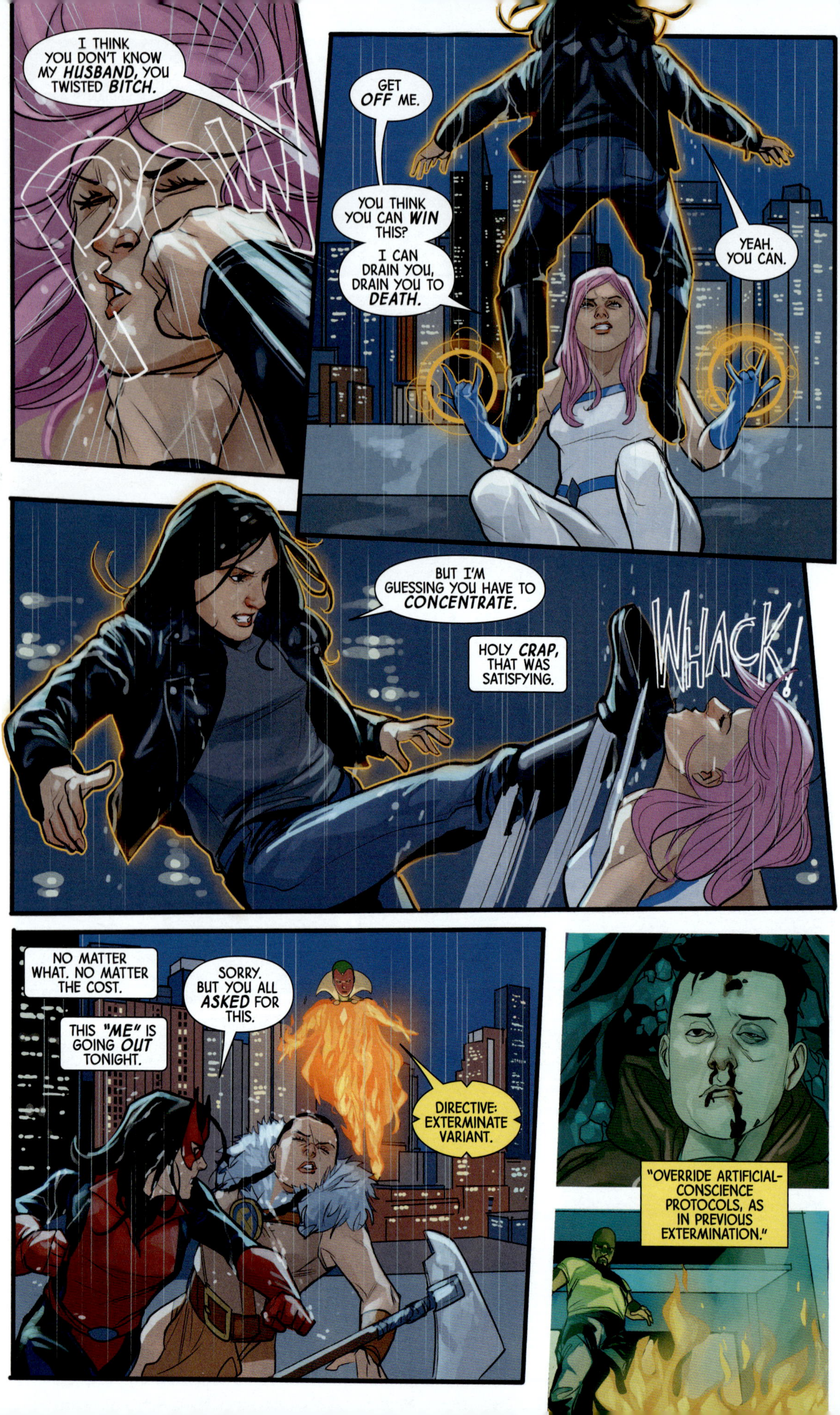
I THINK YOU DON'T KNOW MY *HUSBAND*, YOU TWISTED *BITCH*.
POW
GET *OFF* ME.
YOU THINK YOU CAN *WIN* THIS?
I CAN DRAIN YOU, DRAIN YOU TO *DEATH*.
YEAH. YOU CAN.
BUT I'M GUESSING YOU HAVE TO *CONCENTRATE*.
HOLY *CRAP*, THAT WAS SATISFYING.
WHACK!
NO MATTER WHAT. NO MATTER THE COST.
THIS *"ME"* IS GOING *OUT* TONIGHT.
SORRY. BUT YOU ALL *ASKED* FOR THIS.
DIRECTIVE: EXTERMINATE VARIANT.
"OVERRIDE ARTIFICIAL-CONSCIENCE PROTOCOLS, AS IN PREVIOUS EXTERMINATION."

CHIK
YEAH. NO.
WE DON'T HAVE TO DO THIS. DO YOU NOT SEE THAT?
WE TEAM UP. WE SEND YOU HOME.
BAM
SOME OF US DON'T HAVE A HOME ANYMORE.
KAPOW
THEY HAVE US BEAT--TWO TO ONE, CAP. WE CAN'T WIN.
WE WILL WIN.
KNOW HOW I KNOW?

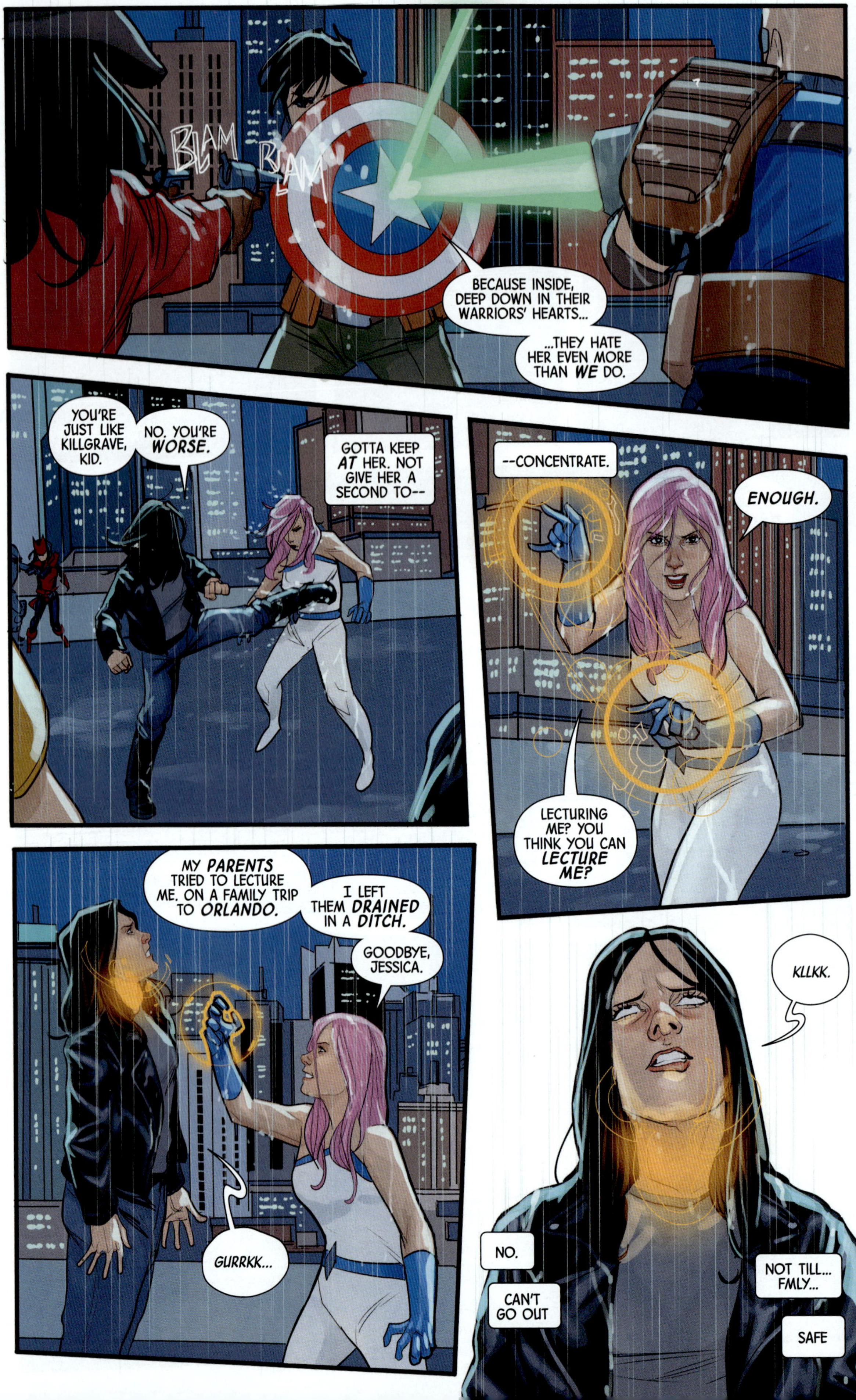
BLAM BLAM
BECAUSE INSIDE, DEEP DOWN IN THEIR WARRIORS' HEARTS...
...THEY HATE HER EVEN MORE THAN WE DO.
YOU'RE JUST LIKE KILLGRAVE, KID.
NO. YOU'RE WORSE.
GOTTA KEEP AT HER. NOT GIVE HER A SECOND TO--
--CONCENTRATE.
ENOUGH.
LECTURING ME? YOU THINK YOU CAN LECTURE ME?
MY PARENTS TRIED TO LECTURE ME. ON A FAMILY TRIP TO ORLANDO.
I LEFT THEM DRAINED IN A DITCH.
GOODBYE, JESSICA.
GURRKK...
KLLKK.
NO.
CAN'T GO OUT
NOT TILL... FMLY...
SAFE

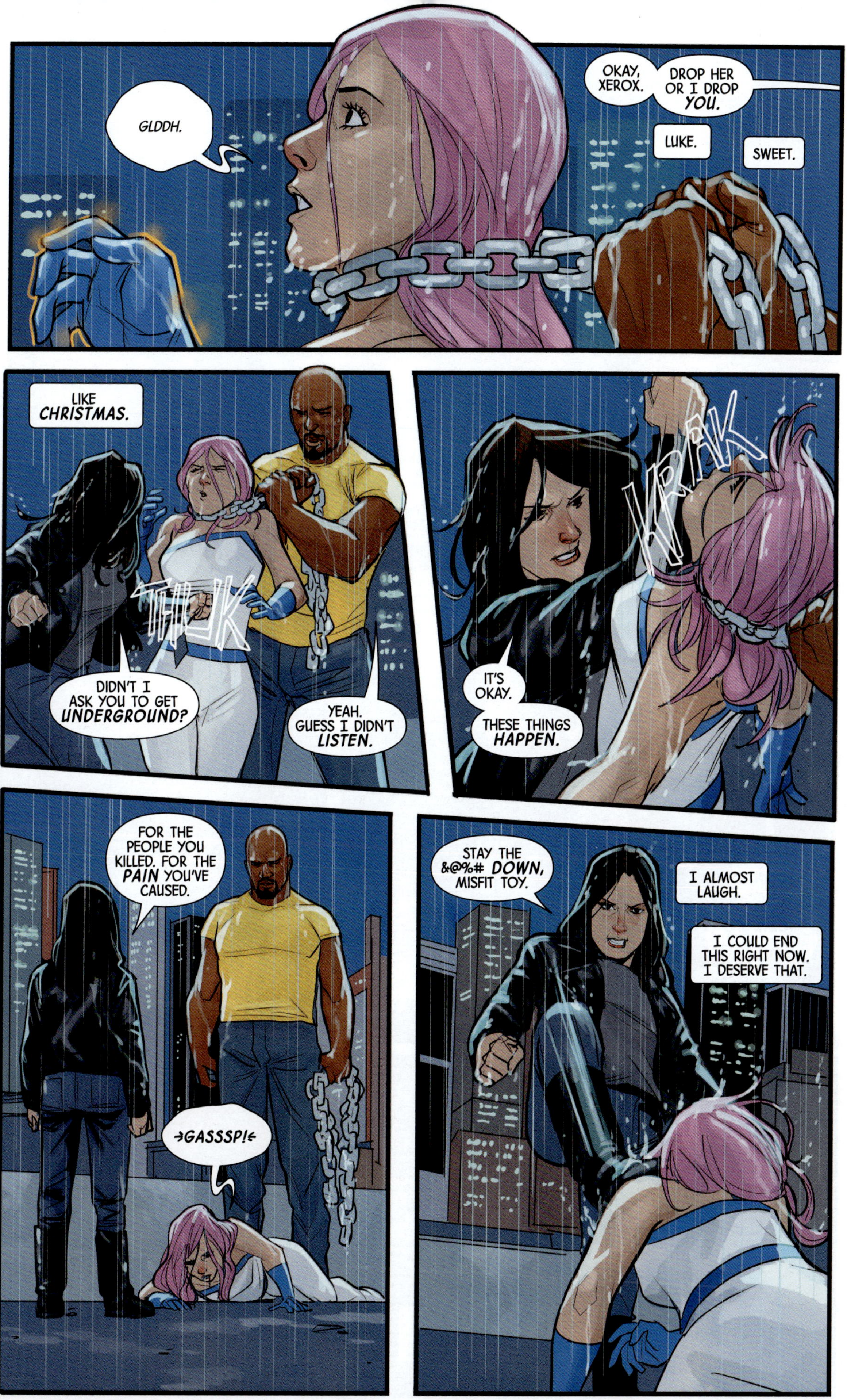
GLDDH.
OKAY, XEROX.
DROP HER OR I DROP YOU.
LUKE.
SWEET.
LIKE CHRISTMAS.
THUK
DIDN'T I ASK YOU TO GET UNDERGROUND?
YEAH. GUESS I DIDN'T LISTEN.
VRAK
IT'S OKAY.
THESE THINGS HAPPEN.
FOR THE PEOPLE YOU KILLED. FOR THE PAIN YOU'VE CAUSED.
GASSSP!
STAY THE &@%# DOWN, MISFIT TOY.
I ALMOST LAUGH.
I COULD END THIS RIGHT NOW. I DESERVE THAT.

BUT IT WOULDN'T MAKE ANY OF THEM WHOLE.
KILL YOU
DRAIN YOU ALL
VARIANTS.
SHE'S DOWN. SHE HAS NO HOLD OVER YOU.
SHE CAN'T DO ANYTHING TO YOU.
HOW ABOUT YOU COME KICK HER ASS FOR HER?
NO. NOOOO!
AND THAT RAIN-SOAKED, SHINING MOMENT...
...IS WHEN A SPOILED LITTLE BRAT LEARNED THE CONSEQUENCES OF TRYING TO PLAY THE ADULT GAME.

THE RAIN STOPPED AND THE CLOUDS PARTED.

I WASN'T SURE IF THAT WAS EVER GOING TO HAPPEN AGAIN.

I THINK THEY DID IT FOR *US*.

JUST WE TWO.

TURNS OUT, KNIGHTRESS DIDN'T GET SUMMONED HERE WITH THE REST. SHE'D BEEN HUNTING THE KILLER.

AND HAD ANOTHER CARPOOL DRIVER ENTIRELY.

HER EARTH'S SORCERER SUPREME. DR. WANDA *STRANGE*.

TURNS OUT KNIGHTRESS WAS DATING HER *BROTHER* OR SOMETHING.

DON'T LOOK AT ME--I NEVER UNDERSTAND WHAT IFS.

THEY COULDN'T LET JEWEL GET CLOSE...THE DANGER OF *STRANGE* BEING DRAINED WAS TOO *HIGH*.

BUT BINDING AN UNCONSCIOUS SERIAL KILLER, THAT WAS RIGHT IN HER WEIRD *WHEELHOUSE*.

REGRET SUBROUTINE ENGAGED. REMORSE IN OVERDRIVE.

WHAT SHE'S TRYIN' TUH SAY, IS WE...WE RECKON WE'RE POWERFUL SORRY, MA'AM. THAT THERE SIDEWINDER, SHE--

I KNOW.

JUST GO. TRY TO LIVE A LIFE THAT *MEANS* SOMETHING.

AND THAT SEEMED LIKE IT. ALMOST A HAPPY ENDING.

ALL THINGS CONSIDERED.

WAIT. SHE DOESN'T-- SHE DOESN'T *HAVE* IT.

WHERE'S THE EYE?

OH NO. SISTER. DON'T.

WHERE'S THE *EYE OF AGAMOTTO*?

OMEGA.

OKAY. LISTEN. JUST LISTEN.

SHE DROPPED IT. I JUST...I JUST GRABBED IT.

I DIDN'T THINK, OKAY?

I'M NOT *LIKE* HER. I DON'T...I DON'T WANT TO TAKE ANYTHING FROM ANYONE.

I JUST...

I JUST WANT MATT.

PLEASE.

IS THAT SO WRONG? IS THAT--?

JESSICA. PLEASE.

WILL YOU SWITCH LIVES WITH ME?

SHE'S GOING TO OPEN A PORTAL.
SHE COULD DESTROY EVERYTHING!
STAND DOWN, LADY.
GIVE HER THIS MOMENT.
OMEGA. JESSICA.
YOU LOST EVERYTHING ONCE AND REBUILT.
I SWEAR. YOU CAN DO IT AGAIN.
I THOUGHT.
I THOUGHT I SAW A LIGHT.
I KNOW.
I'M SORRY.
I'M SO SORRY.

AND THEN THEY WERE GONE.

SOMETIMES YOU WIN, AND SOMEONE ELSE LOSES.

SOMEONE WHO DIDN'T DESERVE IT.

DAWN'S COMING.

IT'S HERE ALREADY.

YOU GOING TO EXPLAIN WHAT HAPPENED, MAYBE?

AND SOMETIMES, YOU FEEL THAT HURT FOR A LONG, LONG TIME.

COME SIT HERE, LIKE WHEN WE WERE COURTING.

"COURTING"? THAT'S WHAT YOU CALL IT?

MR. SARCASM. LUKE, I HAVE SOMETHING TO TELL YOU.

I DECIDED I DON'T WANT TO BE ANYBODY ELSE. NO TWO HUNDRED SHADES OF RED. NO GIRLY PINK.

I JUST WANT TO BE JESSICA.

JESSICA, YOU THINK I DON'T KNOW WHAT THAT MEANS.

I DO.

AND I'M GOOD. I'M IN. FOR THE LONG HAUL.

SHE'LL FIND HER LIGHT, JESS.

I DON'T SAY ANYTHING.

HE'S NEVER REALLY *LOST* ANYONE.

NOT EVEN HIMSELF.

I SAY A QUIET LITTLE PRAYER INSTEAD.

OH, LOOK.

MORNING BLUSH.

THE END.

#1 VARIANT BY **BEN CALDWELL**

#1 VARIANT BY **ASHLEY WITTER**

#1 VARIANT BY **SKOTTIE YOUNG**

#2 VARIANT BY **IVAN SHAVRIN**

#3 VARIANT BY **BETSY COLA**